LOOKING FOR LOVE IN ALL THE WRONG AND RIGHT PLACES

BY

JUDI MCMAHON

ISBN: 0615631681

ISBN 13: 9780615631684

DEDICATION

First I want to thank Bill W. and all his friends for teaching me how to live a more enriched and responsible life through the 12 Steps. I also want to express my gratitude to all the luminous people who have come into my life and helped make it so extraordinary. What a privileged road I've traveled. Thank you Lord.

This book is dedicated to my daughter, Valentina, who after all is said and done and lived, turned out to be the greatest love of my life. God Bless You Real Good, my darling.

"Take me or leave me; or, as is the usual order of things, both."

— DOROTHY PARKER

....

CHAPTER ONE

The White Sands Motel in Amagansett, on the South Fork of Long Island

Summer 2011

Oh no, not again!

Please, Roger, enough already," Tessa muttered. She was hesitant to insult him, but the situation was rapidly deteriorating.

I mean, really, what is it with this idiot? – I meet him at the party; he's like the best catch there – handsome, rich, eligible – a polo player, who once swam on the U.S. Olympic team –Roger Swanson's name is always being mentioned on Page Six hanging out with movie stars and socialites. His handsome image is always front and center in photos snapped at socialite events that make it into Vanity Fair – why, even his home in the Hamptons made Architectural Digest last month. Well – he asked me to leave with him, but soon after – he proceeds to get himself totally smashed, and now he's become just sloppy.

He said he was too drunk to drive safely. That was true. He needed to catch a nap. That was also true. But this was beginning to turn into just another dating disaster! Before Tessa could ponder what to do, Roger had pulled over to a high priced road-side motel. How insulting was that! His Hamptons home was just 20 minutes away. But she did have to get him out of the car into a room rather than risk a terrible driving accident. And now instead of sleeping it off, he was mauling her. Sure Mr. Swanson was drop-dead handsome, yes, he was very, very rich, but that didn't give him the right to take such liberties. Tessa McMullan wouldn't put up with this shabby treatment.

This was turning out to be a huge mistake.

"A" Mistake? Oh no. Tessa had to admit it: this was by no means an uncommon incident, but rather one more mix-up in a series of mistakes! For sure, one shouldn't date the men played up on *Page Six* – they were usually crazy – glamorous, but crazy. It was all about looking for love in all the wrong places.

What was it about Tessa McMullan that attracted these blowhards who seemed to play from the same deck of cards – all about false promises on living happily-ever-after? Was there something wrong with her that lead to nights like this? Roger Swanson's behavior was really dreadful. What happened to his manners – or rather lack of them? He really seemed so charming at the beginning of the evening. She'd never heard any negative gossip about him…that he might have a drinking problem. So how did this happen?

Tessa was truly disgusted. She was weary of men who seemed so nice at first hello, and then turned out to be total creeps, (or, as her mother used to warn her) – *wolves in sheep's clothing*. It hurt to keep meeting up with disappointment. Yet nights like tonight, they were temporary blips on the radar screen – easy to get over compared to the real downers.

For if the truth was to be known, Tessa had her share of heartbreak. Like falling head over heels in love with Teddy Pearson, (such a terrific guy, so charming and good looking, another *Page Six* item, never mind his super career on Wall Street). She was madly in love and just as certain that Teddy was going to propose marriage. Then, suddenly, six months into their romance, (when she was already planning their wedding, though he didn't know it), he revealed that he'd heard from Julie Taylor, his previous girl friend, whose father was a CEO of a large corporation; *(he realized they should never have*

2

broken up, so thank you and good bye). Teddy got a bride and an executive job in her father's corporation. Oh my God, did that hurt.

Then there was Ryan Booth. Now Ryan was really something. Handsome as hell, super rich and powerful with his own popular disco club in Manhattan, but Ryan – he was an absolute control freak. Tessa had met him on of all places, an Internet personal site. He looked and sounded good and for about a month he swept her off her feet with flowers and gifts and a charming gift of gab. But once she saw how dominating he could be, how much he had to control everything, she began retreating. Then it happened – he was doing a line of coke and wanted her to join in….she wouldn't –. This wasn't the first time he'd asked her. Drugs were a no no for Tessa. Besides, she was getting turned off to his bad habit. "No, I don't want any!" she said.

Then things got uglier. He suddenly slapped her across the face; hit her real hard. She realized he was high on coke, it was one of the reasons she was tiring of him, but to attack her – no way – that was too much for Tessa. In fact, Tessa was so offended at Ryan's despicable behavior, she took her shoe (which was a sling back and easy on and off!) and slung it at him, hitting him across the face. She grabbed her handbag and ran out the door. That was that. Or so she thought. Ryan was not the forgive and forget type.

In fact, since that night Ryan's actions grew more bizarre. First he showed up unannounced at her apartment door, banging loudly, insisting he wanted to talk. She wouldn't open the door. He continued to call her, to send flowers and notes of apology. Tessa didn't want to deal with him any longer. Then weeks of hang-ups, and of late, a queasy feeling that she was being followed. She and Ryan Booth were definitely over. So why wouldn't he take no for an answer? He could certainly have his pick of women.

Now what was going on here with Roger Swanson? Was this yet another bad news date? Why was she the only one having so many problems with finding love?

While she kept a glib face on for her friends, Tessa spent many an evening playing old torch songs sung by Sinatra and Garland, the kind where you could cry your heart out and sip maybe one too many wines. And just how many times had she felt sorry for herself when she played Barbara Cook's version of *"Mr. Right Left."* Looking, looking, looking. *Oh please, dear God, why can't I find love?*

For certain – it wasn't to be realized on this weekend in the Hamptons. Tessa bit her lower lip and swallowed hard. Her throat was parched dry. What an awful feeling – all dressed up and nowhere to go but out of here, home.

When she was introduced to Roger Ross Swanson, heir to the oil rich fields his grandfather discovered in Oklahoma, she was thrilled. But that was at Sissy Finnegan's birthday party at the Southampton Yacht Club an historic 4 hours ago.

"Hello, lovely lady, want to dance?" he asked with a sly, off-center grin. He looked like a young Jack Nicholson, sharp, sure of himself, very handsome. Thought a good deal of himself, too. Well, with his family connections and his hunky image, he had every reason to feel confident.

Tessa was told she was an extraordinarily beautiful young lady; long, glistening blonde hair that resembled silken tresses in an old Breck shampoo ad (no wonder she was booked for two hair ads through her modeling agency); wonderful violet blue eyes, an inviting smile and a stunning well-shaped body. She had no problems attracting men. But she was also discerning, wanted more than a bankbook, or a popular jock type – she wanted the whole package. Maybe she was too much of a romanticist. But there she was, still out there, taking risks all over again.

The music played on and on. Roger took her hand, walked her out to the dance floor and held her just a little too close, while the disc jockey spun an old Bee Gee's song from 1969 –(before she was even born,) *"I've Gotta Get A Message To You."* By the time they tripped the light fantastic to another Bee Gee's hit, *"How Do You Mend a Broken Heart?"* Tessa was swooning, feeling a lot like Ginger Rogers dancing with Fred Astaire. Wow, he was smooth.

"Hey, let's drive over to the Surfside Inn; it's in Montauk – not far from here," he suggested. Good, already Roger wanted to be alone with her. And even better, she wouldn't have to dance any longer, since her brand new Jimmy Choo heels were beginning to pinch her big toe.

They raced over to the eatery in his ultra sexy silver Ferrari LWB California Spyder, a real collector's item and one of only 49 made. That was impressive. They dined out on the veranda. Correction: *Drank* out on the veranda. By this time Tessa was feeling ditsy after her third *Dirty Martini*, never mind all the champagne she had imbibed earlier at the party, while Roger had downed twice that number and soon was smashed out of his handsome gourd.

Damn it, he realized – I shouldn't have taken the allergy medication – hay fever or not. Roger wasn't stupid; he knew drink and pills didn't mix. So why had he made this dumb mistake? Once he had accepted the first glass of champagne, reasoning went out the window. He had another and another and now in his muddled-up state, he was behaving like an idiot, but couldn't seem to stop himself. He was woozy and his thinking was way off. It was too late; he was having an allergic reaction.

And now here she was in this rather uncompromising position. In of all places –a motel room. Not fair. Not right. Tessa McMullan, all petite 120 pounds of her, was fed up with this obviously spoiled playboy, all six feet two inches of him trying to get her to lie down with him. She didn't realize he was besotted because of his taking antihistamine medication. Enough already!

And what about his $2 million vacation home in Easthampton – the one she had seen in *Town & Country Magazine?* What the heck was she doing here in a motel room nearby, albeit one that cost $300 for the night? True it was right off the road and he was in no condition to drive, but still she didn't want to be there at all! Tessa felt hurt, taken advantage of, damn it all, wronged again!

Fortunately it wasn't too long before he passed out – like three minutes – and soon began snoring. This handsome young man with the immense fortune was snoring. *What next? This is a disaster*, she realized. She had to get away.

No – not for all the money in the world, not for his ski home in Telluride, his Fifth Avenue co-op, his apartment in Rome (Tess had done her homework well), was this sought-after bachelor the right one for her. She tip toed across the darkened room quietly, searched around for her prized Jimmy Choo shoes, heard him call out: "Hey Tessa baby, come here, come on to bed," and decided to forget about the other shoe, grabbed her Prada handbag and ran out the door.

She had enough money and credit cards on her to call a taxi from the front office. Tessa limped hurriedly over the cobblestone path, scraping her left toe, but didn't dare stop or look back. She was making her great escape. And feeling just awful. It was dreadful to have her dreams shattered once again. And while it was only Saturday morning, she had to get back to the city and out of the motel parking lot. Her big toe and her ego were equally hurting. Disappointed, missing one pricey shoe, Tessa headed back – back to square one. Come to think of it – wasn't it Tracy Martin – her old college roommate, who said there just weren't any decent and available men in New York? She did move on, all the way to Seattle, where Tracy soon reported, she met the perfect man in a mere three weeks? Darn it, Tessa didn't know what to do!

Thank God it was Sunday. Tessa stretched her gorgeous body so lithe, so like a cat, across her creamy cotton Porthault sheets and gazing at the reflection in the mirror (strategically placed across from her bed), admired her beautiful self. Long blonde hair, platinum highlights, full lips, the right nose and a to-die-for body. She knew she was a knock out; that men were attracted to her. Even though Roger Swanson was eminently qualified he certainly didn't fit the role of a knight in shining armor. He was a drunk. Too bad. After that scene in the motel room, Tessa considered him more like one of the frogs that you had to kiss until the Prince came along. She was afraid she'd become like many New York women. They married their careers.

Tessa took a fleeting look at the clock radio. Merd! It was already noon. She was to meet the girls at the Rihga Royal for brunch in an hour. They convened at least twice monthly. Summer time was tricky with some in the Hamptons, others traveling. This weekend they had planned on Manhattan, so it was just as well she'd come back early.

She bounded out of bed, rushed to get ready and soon was on the street hoping to hail a taxi cab cross town to W. 54th Street, where she could tell the girls her latest adventure. (Of course, she'd leave out the part where she was really crushed by the experience.) She knew how to put on a happy face. Tessa loved these get-togethers – the opportunity to be the star! Wait until they hear about her meeting Roger Swanson – their jaws will drop with jealousy!

"Taxi! Here," she waved. The Checker cab stopped and she hopped right in. Out of the corner of her eye Tessa noticed a figure standing in the doorway, some man who seemed to be watching her.

"Tell him I was too fucking busy– or vice versa."

— DOROTHY PARKER

CHAPTER TWO

The Rihga Royal was an ultra elegant hotel on West 54th Street with rooms starting at $265 a night. Definitely on the *"A"* list of where-to-brunch. Never mind you never knew who you'd meet in the plush marble lobby or at the bar in the evening.

"Kisses, kisses," Tessa greeted her comrades, seated at a booth. Vera Stern-Klinghower, dressed in a knock-out Versace purple pantsuit that flattered her figure (and the latest Manolo Bhalnick's daring ankle-chain sandals) kissed-kissed her back first.

"Wow, don't you look fantastic!" commented Angel Manelli, on the plump side, and clad in a black dress by Gucci. Poor Angel, from her prepubescent days at the Mountain Valley school, she'd always been a chubby child and still waged a losing battle to whittle down her weight. She couldn't help but envy Tessa's size 4 figure. But while Angel packed on extra poundage, she still knew how to accessorize (and hopefully take the focus off her fat). Today the camouflage gear was an oversized $1,600 Dolce and Gabbana handbag she proudly carried.

Of course, Tessa was dressed for success in a ravishing red Hermes feather-light lambskin dress, (the better to show off her great body) and brand new Jimmy Choo heels. No one would fail to notice her; no never.

Angel quickly arose from the posh velvet booth to make room for Tessa to slide in; Tessa was their leader and had to be the center of attention, of course.

"You look divine, as usual," Vera complimented Tessa. She knew Tessa would be wearing the best *schmatte* of the group. The trio would always wriggle their tushes into the best of designer clothes, but Tessa, she was so damned competitive that she almost always won the high fashionista award.

"Considering what a simply awful experience I had out in Amagansett Friday evening, and….."

"Oh," Angel squeaked, leaning in, "tell us all about it."

"But, wait…didn't you say Katy would join us?" Vera asked.

"So where is my big sister?" Tessa complained. "She's always always late," she added brusquely, not waiting for a response. Actually it was a rare event for Katy to show up at one of these brunches. She really wasn't a charter member of their group; she had her own life, work and agenda.

"Well she's gotta get here from way downtown, so let's give her another five minutes," Angel suggested. She'd always liked Katy, and secretly thought she was the much nicer of the two sisters, but naturally, kept her opinion to herself. "And Vera, your outfit is absolutely phenomenal!"

Well, thank you for the compliment, Angel. They say purple is a royal color – and I was feeling royal this morning. So how are we doing?" Vera asked, drinking a little bit more of her second mimosa. If the truth were known, she had started imbibing at home with vodka and orange juice just to dull the boredom she felt at her equally boring husband who snored loudly beside her much of the night. Who cared if he was an eminent cardiologist in town, he was a drag in bed with a penis the size of a peanut.

"Who was it that said that the average woman would rather have beauty than brains because she knows that the average man can see much better than he

can think?" Tessa proffered. "Here, here!" Vera agreed. Yes, Tessa knew her "A" Team, this gorgeous trio who always dressed to the nines, would agree with her.

"Ta Da! I had a real clunker Friday night. Wasted a good evening with none other than Roger Swanson!" The women leaned in – Swanson was a really great catch and if Tessa didn't like him, with all his millions, there had to be something utterly wrong with him.

Soon enough there were laughs and titters among them, as they listened to Tessa's raunchy retelling of her Friday night calamity, (she still mourned her lost shoe) so much so that the women didn't notice Katy McMullan approaching the booth.

Tall at 5'7", stunning with an aquiline nose, Irish dimples, and a perky short hairdo, it wouldn't be too evident to a stranger that this beautiful young woman was gay. Dressed in a Ralph Lauren pale beige cashmere sweater with ultra sleek gabardine slacks, she just looked a little sportier than the haute couture trio that greeted her.

"Well hello, big sister," Tessa said, and not so subtly glaring at Katy, looked her over head to toe. Damn it why didn't she wear any makeup? How many times did she tell her that at the least, lipstick was a MUST?

Tessa considered herself a modern woman, tolerant of the "L" word people, and of course, admired a host of gay men who contributed much to our culture – from Stephen Sondheim to Calvin Klein – she knew they were ultra talented. But deep down, somewhere inside, she was still uncomfortable with her sister's alternative lifestyle. But if the truth were to be known, her real resentment was in how Katy had made such a great career for herself, and didn't even finish college, while she, Tessa, was struggling to make it. It just wasn't fair.

Tessa remembered the prestigious event when Katy revealed to her family that she was gay. She'd come home that Thanksgiving weekend with a new "friend" and there, right after dinner, she revealed to their parents that she had met someone special and that special someone was a woman, her dinner guest! The one who owned a flower shop and had brought them that fabulous centerpiece for the holiday table.

Tessa was annoyed. Never mind that Katy was working in the much admired New York City Crime Scene Unit – No less as a detective, and glory be! Now she also had a partner who owned her own business. Why did Katy seem to get all the breaks?

Never mind, Katy was a good story teller, and Tessa had to admit, she had some darn good stories to tell. She'd be the first to applaud Katy's spirit and wit. Being a woman and making it to detective in the chauvinistic male police department was a major feat in itself. It really wasn't easy for Katy McMullan, nor did she ever forget her struggle to make it. On most of the rare occasions when she met with the girls, they always asked for more anecdotes knowing she could weave a yarn guaranteed to amuse them.

"How about a story based on one of your many experiences?" Vera asked. "Your tales are truly captivating!"

"I admit to having war stories about my years on the job that would get your antennas up, ladies," Katy laughed.

"So come on, tell us one," Angel implored.

"Well….okay. I know a light one – not too much angst in it. I'm thinking back to before I even made detective and was still on part time foot patrol out in Queens. I was just finishing up eating lunch. I was in the radio car with my part-ner, who incidentally was not cheerful about being paired with a female. A little guy, all flustered and red in the face, he runs up to the squad car and says he was robbed at gunpoint and furthermore the robber is running through the park across the street. So me and my partner John (who, may I remind you, was not very happy hanging out with me, a woman, even in a job situation) – anyway – we know we are going to have to investigate. Now, John was a big man – 6'3" and weighed in about 260 pounds. We pack up our lunches (slowly) and drive to where the man said he was robbed. And lo and behold there is this angry looking guy in the park running quickly – so John and I get out to give chase."

"I am going from tree to tree tracking the guy. Now there is a path he is on. I see him throw something down. I make a mental note; maybe it's the victim's wallet. We're still in hot pursuit. Now we are approaching the edge of the park. He turns on me and my partner with a gun in his hand. I run behind this huge tree and John, he's behind a sapling!! Big tree, little tree. John looks at me and says "what's wrong with this picture?" Anyway, we can't shoot at him, there's traffic behind him and if we miss we kill someone innocent! So we run after him. John tackles him, I retrieve the gun, a loaded 380 automatic and then I walk back to where I saw him throw something down and recover a loaded 45. No wallet, however. That was still on him. Good collar. But big tree, little tree. The lesson learned: Proper planning prevents piss poor performance. And looking back, one of us could have been hit."

Beautiful! You're a hoot," Tessa said. "And incidentally, I've never heard that one before."

"Wow, Katy, you certainly were in perilous situations. I sometimes fail to remember that you have this horribly dangerous job that none of us could do," Vera noted. You really are a heroine!"

Katy smiled. "Thanks, hon. Frankly, I was glad myself to get off the regular beat and finally make detective. The pay is damned good and the work more challenging."

"Mom, Dad, we were all thrilled when you got it, sis," Tessa said with pride in her sister's success.

"When all's said and done, it wasn't that easy getting there. Tricky actually. I was fortunate; I made detective in seven years. Most cops – it takes ten to twelve years. When I was transferred to the Crime Scene Unit the commanding officer from that unit said he received no less than twenty calls, from sergeants to chiefs and even the police commissioner's office – all putting in a good word for me. This meant a lot to me. And I never ever take my duties for granted. I'm lucky to have the good job that I do!"

"And I know it's far from easy for you, sis, that you work long hours, sometimes double shifts. You need special emotional stamina to do it," Tessa praised her sister. It had taken a long time for her to get there, but the admiration that she now felt for Katy was real. Tessa was beginning to mature and finally appreciate what an immense battle it was for her big sister to overcome the prejudices of the past decades to homosexuality. Slowly — perhaps not until 2000 and after — was their gradual acceptance of individuals who sought same sex relationships. Not only did she handle this with grace, but Katy also overcame the incessant prejudices of male cops and detectives in accepting women as their equals. She served on the largest municipal police force in the United States, There presently are over 37,000 on the NYPD force and only 17% of these are women. Darn it, Tessa realized, Katy was a stand-up broad!

"Well, sometimes it's easy and a lot of times it's not. I suppose my worst moment was when my partner and I had to be one of the first responders to the Twin Towers on 9/11. I made it out of there alive; she didn't. It still haunts me."

"Geeze...I almost forgot this, Katy. I remember being told that you were called down there that very morning. Tessa had phoned and we both wondered where you were, and when we learned that you were on duty that day, we just knew you were there. We all did a lot of praying that day. Thank God you made it," Angel said.

"That's why Katy now gets called for special investigative work," Tessa whispered. "You were down in New Mexico last October with the FBI, right?"

"Yeah, the department paid for me to go there and participate in a series of bombing tests out in the desert. We were there to observe what would happen to buildings and cars when they were bombed. Of course, this was under controlled circumstances, but being a "first responder" – they felt my expertise would come in handy.

"I'm sure it did. Let's just hope we're safer now in the city," Vera said.

"I'm afraid I wouldn't count on it. I hope I'm wrong, but there may be an attempt to bomb a bridge or a tunnel or get to to the subways sometime in late 2012 or 2013. They're sick, demented and they're not going to give up. They want to keep terrorizing us and the only way to do this and to affect the economy too, is to hit us again," Katy said gravely.

"As if our economy, never mind the world situation, isn't a total disaster these days!" Vera said. "You don't know where to put your money these days...that is if you have any."

"Forget about it, ladies. Let's all have a drink before we depart," Katy suggested. "We're going to make it; things have to get better. Our country will be okay. It just has to."

Tessa had to agree with her sister. Nevertheless, there was still that tiny bit of envy; she had always felt that their father favored Katy. As long as she could remember, Katy was "Daddy's little girl." That still bothered her.

And while Tessa would never admit it to her friends she was still a bit envious of her sister holding what one had to admit was an authentically thrilling job; never mind one that paid her over $100,000 a year. And she had also found love, someone with whom to share her life. Meanwhile she was still out there looking, never mind still struggling to find her way as an actress, and she couldn't figure out why. Perhaps it was time to reconsider what she wanted and what she needed; there was a difference. She was beautiful and she was smart and she was talented, yet Hollywood had never noticed. One small part in a soap opera was all she could claim. And worse, she still hadn't found *"Mr. Right,"* What she really hoped to find was a man she could respect, not some playboy or shallow individual. She'd had her fill of them.

Worse, it was painfully evident that their father still preferred Katy, no matter what her way of life.

Why did Katy seem so happy, so content with her life? Sometimes Tessa would cry herself to sleep. What was she doing so wrong? Something was out of kilter. Tessa wanted total acceptance, to be admired and respected. And in the world as she saw it – that reverence came from finding the right husband. She was hell-bent on getting herself a *real* man, someone to wine her and dine her and sweep her off her well-heeled feet – all the way to the ALTAR. And of course, for them to live happily ever after like all the wistful books and movies promised.

She'd had so many false starts, misadventures – she was really not very happy with her lack of success with men. What was wrong with her? She never shared all her secrets with her friends, especially the disaster with Ryan Booth. Ryan seemed to have everything when she had first met him, great looks, a fabulous business as the owner of a hot disco club, and women all over the place wanting to be on his *"A"* list. But Ryan honed right in on Tessa. At the beginning, she was pleased with all of his flattery and near-fanatical attention. Roses arrived daily; he sent a limo to pick her up for their dates, even though the limo was only driving her ten blocks west to his club, "Blast!". Gifts, so many of them, were bought for her and were so expensive that Tessa was starting to feel a little suffocated by all the attentiveness. There was nothing Ryan wouldn't do to make sure that Tessa was happy.

But she wasn't. Ryan had too many issues; mainly his need for cocaine and his stronger need to control. This wasn't going to work out. Once again, she'd have to look elsewhere. Not to worry. She knew it wouldn't be easy finding "Mr. Right," yet she was confident. Tessa wasn't going to settle for anything less than the best, the decent man she deserved. Lately, she was growing far more cautious and wise; she knew money was far from the top of the list of what was important.

Look out world! I'm beautiful and smart and I'm going to get what I want come hell or high water. Tessa wasn't giving up, no way! She was determined to succeed.

> Accept that some days you're the pigeon, and some days you're the statue.
>
> (UNKNOWN)

....

CHAPTER THREE

(Headline story in NY Daily Planet, August 7, 2012)

Gunplay horror! Girl shot in eye by boy in B'klyn

An 11-year-old city girl was in critical condition last night after she was shot in the face by a pal who thought the gun was a toy, the victim's devastated father said.

It was an unusually hot August day; so scorching that as Tessa crossed Lexington Avenue, the black tar pavement was softening beneath her feet. She had to rescue one of her 4 inch Ralph Lauren wedgies from the blistering path. At the corner of 59th Street the newsstand featured not only newspapers and magazines, but a rack laden with tourist *chotchkes* like the latest designer sunglass knock-offs. The tabloid headlines featured the up-to-the-minute horror stories of the city but Tessa McMullan was oblivious to most of what went on around her. After all, she needed a new *uniform* for her latest evening competition. Too bad she wasn't more observant, because she might have noticed that this very creepy looking man with a hard look to him had been following her down the street. He stopped when she entered the department store, but still, what was he doing following her in the first place? It would be a very long time before Tessa learned the answer.

"Listen, honey bun," Tessa purred fallaciously at her sister. (Multi-tasking as usual, she was chatting into her cell phone while rummaging through a designer sale rack at Bloomie's.) *Some sale! The sweaters began at $400, and the dresses had price tags starting at $800. Phooey! She had an opening to go to – last minute thing – heard Leonardo DiCaprio and Matt Damon were going to be there. She absolutely had to wear something spectacular. What the hell. She'd posed for that super sexy negligee shot for Playboy which allowed her $1,000 extra wardrobe money. (Too bad that she was a cup size away from a centerfold – the real big time.) She was actually thinking about larger implants, but that was costly too.*

"Now, what was I saying? – oh yes," Tessa implacable, as always, continued. "I go out of my way to include you in our merry little goings-on. After all, *"The Bod Squad"* – (her pet name for the group) – *every* one of us – – we all love seeing you."

"And I like seeing all of you, I.….."

Tessa cut her sister off at the pass: "But why, why, *every* rare time you show up do you have to show up looking like you stood against the wall and someone threw your clothes on?" I mean, the Rihga is tres chic and there we were at a really good booth, in the center of the room with all eyes upon us – and only you looked…well, not *au courant*," she droned on disdainfully. Actually she held back from what she really thought, because Katy was always underdressed, boring looking simply out of style! If Tessa could have said what she really wanted to when she saw her that day it would have been: "You look like shit. Is that the style now?"

But she knew it was a no-win situation, that Katy would not change a hair on her head, nor heed any of her good advice.

"Tessy, why are you always bitching about how I look?" Katy snapped back. She was weary of being lectured to by her pain-in-the-ass kid sister. *Go ahead, stupid, rant and rave, call me a "plain Jane," say whatever you want.*

Sticks and stones may break my bones, but names will never harm me. God, that was something she said when she was ten years old – could her feelings go back that far?

"*Why* is a crooked letter," Tessa bantered. "You know I'm not the only one that thinks you could dress up a bit more. Mom was always telling you to play up your pretty face, and you never ever listened to her either."

But clothing, makeup, this had little to do with Tessa's real antipathy. She couldn't help it; it really bothered her that her sister was doing so well with her career while she was still floundering.

"Back off! You're standing in my aura," Katy shot back. She could be as sarcastic as the next one.

"Alright, I really don't want to argue with you. I know you've chosen your lifestyle, and while it's not what I would do, hey, it's your life."

"*Fuck it! What's the use,*" Katy realized. This was an endless conflict. No, it was more like a war! For some reason her sister believed she was entitled to tell anyone within her purview what to do. Katy wanted no part of Tessy's overbearing ways. Yet, it was her fault too. Chrissie would remind her of how her sister could push her buttons, yet, she'd stay away for months only to once again accept an invitation and sure enough – catch more of this crap. But while Katy could keep up a good front, tell amusing anecdotes, banter with the best of them – it hurt. Sometimes (but always when no one could see her) she'd be reduced to tears. She felt the lack of acceptance had to do with her sexual orientation. Not fair. But then life wasn't supposed to be fair, was it?

"*Detective McMullan, Detective McMullan;*" Tessa could hear her sister being paged on the intercom at the CSU division where she worked. Damn, at least she had a good job; she couldn't take that away from Katy. Well the Crime Scene Unit was one place *where people were dying to meet her*!

"Oh to hell with it Tessy, I don't need your approval for how I dress – for anything. Gotta go. Later." SLAM!

Katy had hung up the phone. Damned if you do and damned if you don't. Her sister acted like she had a pole stuck up her ass with all her high falutin fashion ideas. How one dressed, that was such superficial bullshit. Never mind lately Tessy looked more like a hooker than a sometime soap opera actress. When Chrissie and Katy went to spend time with the family in Larchmont last Christmas, Tessy was dressed up more than the Christmas tree. All she needed was a few light bulbs and they could have put the gifts around her.

Honestly she looked tacky, no matter what designer label she was wearing. Her garb was over the edge, an emerald green dress with ridiculous red and green spangles all over the bodice, never mind the skirt was far too short (the better to show off her shapely legs,) a dyed-to-match emerald mink hat that made her look like she just got off the boat from Vladivostok, and those high heeled boots she wore trudging through the snow were absolutely dim-witted.

Yes, it was amazing how Katy could get sucked right back in. It reminded her of the Michael Corleone line in *The Godfather: "Just when I thought I was out, they pull me back in."* Most of the time Katy turned down invitations to join the girls for their weekly Sunday brunch. She had a good excuse; she often worked weekends and double shifts. She even said no to last winter's weekend ski trip that she would have enjoyed. Then she stupidly agreed to meet Tessy and the girls at the Rihga this past Sunday. It didn't take long for the animosity between the sisters to rear its ugly head.

One thing for certain – Tessa abhorred Katy getting (and holding) the girls' attention – but Katy was always a good story teller and this Sunday she was relating a funny event that happened to her when she was still on foot patrol. It happened to concern a chicken! Or as Katy told it:

"Early on in my career, when I was still on foot patrol, I was sitting in Forest Park, in Queens with my partner. We were having our lunch. There was a chicken walking around in the city park! Yes, an honest-to-God real live chicken! So we fed the chicken – I guess someone got a chick for Easter and later set him free in the park. So whenever we happened to be in that park eating lunch, I continued to feed him. This went on for a few weeks.

The girls listened with rapt attention.

Katy continued: *"Well, one day I heard shots fired in the park. Then a teenager came out holding a BB gun. I asked him what he was doing. He said 'I just shot a chicken.' Well firing a BB gun in the city is a violation of the administrative code. I put the cuffs on him. He started rattling off names of cops he knew. I shook my head and laughed at him. I told him: "I knew the Chicken." I went into the park and he had indeed killed that chicken. He was under arrest for various things...possession of a dangerous instrument, violation of the BB gun law, cruelty to animals, unlawful this and that. Name dropping didn't do him any good."*

The bod squad laughed, then applauded. Even Tessa had to smile.

It was really a funny story. And true.

Katy never did understand why her sister could act so headstrong. She was always wanting, wanting, wanting, and worse, getting what she asked for. Like that expensive co-op on Sutton Place their father bought for her. Sure, it was a good buy back in 1998 when the market wasn't off the charts, and James McMullan, a partner in a prestigious Wall Street law firm could certainly afford it, but even that magnanimous endeavor didn't satisfy Tessy. Not at all. Damned if the maintenance wasn't $900 a month and she had to actually *work* to pay for that. Katy knew not to give advice where it wasn't wanted. But Tessa's choice of a career, modeling and acting, had not been working out for her. The girl had a good education; she wished she'd use it.

As for Katy, what the heck did her parents ever give *her*? Yes, her dad was nice enough to her, but he was hardly around all those years she was growing up. He worked long hours at his law office, taking the NY Central commuter train home to Larchmont, often arriving at the front door as late as 10 p.m., long after she was asleep. Then along came Tessa, (Tessy to Katy) and right away, her mother favored her little blonde haired girl. They were different that way too. Tessy was the blonde with blue eyes while Katy had mousy brown hair, though beautiful green eyes. Tessa was naturally slender and petite, while Katy was big boned, and had to watch what she ate.

After high school, and exhausted from the bickering at home, Katy, with her father's backing, moved into a dorm at NYU and never looked back. She was sick and tired of her mother nagging her about her not looking feminine enough; sick and tired of hiding how she really felt. And damned if she didn't end up making it on her own, worked really hard and though they snickered at her quitting NYU after a year to pursue a lowly police career, she knew that's what she wanted to do.

Making it as a New York City cop wasn't easy. To even get accepted into training, she first had to pass a civil service exam. That took plenty of studying too. Then she had to pass rigorous physical exams; sit-ups, push-ups, weight lifting, obstacle courses – the whole wearing, draining, exhausting gamut. Katy sucked at the sit-ups, because she had a tiny little tail bone that was getting raw from doing them. The pain was relentless. She called her uncle, who was on the job since 1976. At that point she wanted to quit. He talked her out of it, saying *this was the hardest she'd ever work for the rest of her career*. Years later she realized, boy was he right.

Then she waited on tenterhooks to see if she passed. After all of these physically draining, mentally exhausting challenges, she still had to kill time. It took her three long years before she went into the academy. She waitressed, worked at odd jobs, tried driving a cab in traffic-congested Manhattan; Jesus, Mary and Joseph, that was the worst.

It was a difficult period – rooming first with a couple of women she had met in a gay bar on Bleecker Street, and then finally finishing up the grueling, demanding six month course at the Police Academy to cross the threshold into lowly rookie status. Not that it happened all at once. About a year after the test Katy received a computer-generated card with her score. Hurrah! She'd more than passed. Then she had to take a physical and then an agility test. Not done yet. Now a damned psychological test. Eventually she got into the academy, where they tell you *"you are lower than whale shit."* Not exactly an ego-builder! Some of the courses there included police science, social science (which was glorified sensitivity training), and law – penal, administrative and traffic law. NYU classes were a breeze compared to the demands of the training.

Oh yeah, once she was hired, she was "on the job," – street work, finally a patrol car, but to make detective – that was a real nut to crack. Most women could wait as long as 15 years or more. Katy lucked out, got good recommendations from her supervisors and then, after waiting three years to get fully investigated she made Detective Third Grade, eight long years after joining the force.

Recalling yesterday's group brunch at the Righa, Katy heaved a sigh. There was a love/hate relationship between her and her sister. Never mind Tessy just calling to criticize what she had worn. Katy flinched as she remembered yet another of her sister's acidic comments from yesterday.

Judi McMahon

"So how come you've never made *first grade* detective?" she asked at the brunch – right in front of their friends, (knowing that this was a rare occurrence anyway).

"Because you need to have a major *hook* – know a chief, someone of high rank – and the others who make it, they're a bunch of ass-kissers. And most of 'em end up *on their backs*. I wouldn't even do a *hand job* to get ahead. And some of the women – they'd stab you right in the back if they thought it would get them first grade. Only about five percent of detectives ever make first grade. I personally would rather keep my dignity and never get first grade. I'm happy where I am."

"You're awe-inspiring," said Angel, "I mean you do serious, important work and wow, you're with CSI – just like that television show with forensics and all those dead bodies – it's so exciting! And that you made detective in the first place – it's all to your credit."

"You go, girl!" echoed Vera.

Tessa had to cover up her true feelings, but the real fact of the matter was her exasperation at Angel's waxing ecstatic about Katy; no less Vera cheering her on! Damned if the girls didn't look up to her sister like some sort of heroine.

"Not true!" Tessa's thoughts flew through her mind with a long ago fury; one that had only festered with time. Hell, Katy did mostly desk work, some investigation, but nothing, no nothing special! But that was just like her older sister – she was always trying to steal the spotlight away from her. Tessa wouldn't allow that. It was bad enough she had to listen to Katy when she was little – she was so bossy! Now, Tessa was doing great herself. And she applauded herself (somebody had to!) – I'm much prettier – have had lots of men interested in me – I had a running role on "General Hospital" for three years. Big fucking deal, so Katy was a cop that was about it. Why did her father always tell everyone about his daughter, the CSU Detective like it was something special? Why didn't her father appreciate all she had achieved and she was only 25!

"Waiter, a little more coffee, please, and the check," Tessa announced. She wanted to end this brunch and NOW.

"I read that great interview you did with the Daily News crime writer. I was so proud to know you," Angel added, oblivious to Tessa's directive.

"Oh my yes…in fact, what you said in that story – it was fan-fucking-tastic!" Vera added with great praise.

Katy smiled. "Thanks. But you know, I was just talking about an awful child abuse case, trying to shed some light on the horrible foster care conditions that led to that two year olds violent death."

"Wow, I wish I had the guts to do your kind of work. Was it easy becoming a detective?"

"It was really quite a battle. I actually should have been considered within the first two years I applied – but the detective who was in the unit that does the background investigation work let my paperwork sit on his desk because he was going through a divorce and totally hated women!"

"So how did you get where you are?" Vera asked with admiration.

"Well lucky for me I had a friend who looked into it and ended up getting me a new investigator."

"Hey, who wants to see the new movie, *"Something borrowed"*? It's playing down the street and I hear it's a riot," interrupted Tessa, wanting to get the focus off her sister.

And within ten minutes, having finished dessert, the girls were off to the movies. Everyone that is, except Katy, who was working a late shift and had to get home and ready.

Hell, sibling rivalry – it started way back when with Cain and Abel. Katy didn't let Tessy's barbs get to her. Besides, she had a good life, a loving companion in Chrissie, and damned if she cared what her sister thought. Or did she?

One impulse from a vernal wood may teach you more of man

Of moral evil and of good than all the sages can

— OSCAR WILDE

CHAPTER FOUR

"Eat your oatmeal, darling," Gisele Swanson urged, as she reached over the table and gently rubbed her son's arm.

"For Christ Sake, mother, I'm a grown man," Roger answered with some irritation.

"When are you going to stop trying to run my life?

"But look at you, so painfully thin and no color in your face. You just don't take care of yourself and I worry."

"I'm absolutely fine. I just had too damned much to drink last night," he admitted, wincing as he recalled waking up at dawn, still in his clothing and in a motel room and, damn it, all alone. How could that McMullan woman run out on him like that? What did he do that was that bad? He didn't have a clue.

Stop! Oh yes he did. He just didn't want to remember taking those damned anti-histamine pills and then drinking on top of that. He knew better than to mix meds with drink. Wow, he'd have to find a way to apologize to that lovely young lady; he knew his behavior was bad.

Roger had driven over to his mother's house in Southhampton, ostensibly to get a cup of coffee; it was closer than his own. But if he had to listen to her go on and on about why he wasn't married yet, why he didn't resume his legal career, all the usual nagging, even for just another minute – he'd put his fist through a wall. Yes, he had a law degree; yes he had put in two ghastly years in corporate law at a prestigious Wall Street law firm. Corporate take over's. He hated every minute of it. So he decided to run his late father's foundations, where he could make a real difference.

He'd chosen as his first project to be of assistance to orphans in Third world countries. Too many had lost their parents to AIDS or other diseases that came with poverty. In the past four years he was responsible for building three orphanages and fully staffing and getting them to run successfully. How was that not work? And his law degree did come in handy; he could read any contract, write his own, and make sure the monies were being spent as the Trustees of the Foundation wanted – for the good of the poor, the disenfranchised. His father's oil fortune now was being put to very good use.

He was annoyed; mostly at himself and his bad manners. Damned if he didn't recognize the truth in his behavior. First, forgetting the common sense rule of never mixing anti-histamines with drink of any kind. Second – getting piss-poor drunk with one too many martinis (and missing the opportunity to spend a pleasurable evening with that luscious blonde). Then, the morning after, it hadn't entered his wet brain to order breakfast in his motel room, nor even to drive back to his Hampton's house. As much as he hated to admit it, he felt an urgent need for immediate relief. And so where else to go? Feeling disappointed and guilty – home to mother. Here he was at 32 still tied to Mommy's apron strings. True, she was a terrific woman and had so many admirable qualities. But why did he still turn to her when he was feeling lousy?

He certainly didn't need his mother for any monetary reason. Roger had total financial security, his own trust fund from the time he turned 25. He really didn't require anything at all from her – advice or emotional support. Besides that, what could he hope to learn from his mother – who could barely live out her own life? But then why did Roger go back to the wrong well, time and time again? For one thing, his mother was a rather sympathetic character, a wounded soul who seemed to have lost her reason for living after his father died. He felt compassion for her because she was misunderstood; his maternal grandmother, now 97 and in a nursing home, had never liked her daughter-in-law, always thought of her as an interloper, but truly Gisele had been a devoted wife and mother. Now, she lived in a netherworld, and far too much in the past.

Gisele Walden Swanson had always claimed an exceptional influence upon her son. She'd become somewhat of a recluse in the past decade, ever since Roger's father had died. She lived alone, with little help, just her trusted housekeeper and two Siamese cats. She rarely made the social scene any longer and had stopped traveling years ago. Gisele spent the summer months in her Southampton home, the rest of the year at her East 60th Street town house. And aside from writing out a check or two each month to favorite charities, (and here she was generous to a fault, giving thousands each month to a shelter for homeless women and also supporting the *Habitat for Humanity* program) but aside from this she involved herself in little outside activities that would give her positive benefits and friends. She seemed to live for her son, while most of the time Roger was impervious to it all.

What really kept Roger connected to his mother was her frail vulnerability. She had been kind and good all the days she raised him, and now, while really not an old woman, she lived like one. Sadly she had recused herself from this world.

Gisele was still an exquisite woman, a cool blonde beauty even without makeup or designer clothes. She was content to wear jeans and casual tops and rarely donned a dress. The 5'7" ex-model was still stunning at 57. She'd met Jonathan Swanson, the heir to the Swanson oil fortune when she was 25 and he was double her age. She'd earned a good income as a high fashion model, but that wasn't enough for her prospective in-laws. There was no doubt that the Swanson family, especially family matriarch, Eleanor Swanson, were certain she was marrying their eldest son for his immense wealth and position. Divorced, no children, lonely, Jonathan was primed for a new marriage and quickly succumbed to Gisele's overwhelming beauty and grace. She would be a prevailing force within the union for the rest of their lives.

And now Gisele still played a leading role in her son's life. Maybe if he didn't end up an only child he'd feel less impelled to account for his deeds. Maybe if his older brother (by four years), Jonathan, Jr., hadn't died in a freak boating accident at the age of eight, his mother wouldn't have made Roger the consuming target of all her benevolence.

It was never easy to escape his mother's protective concerns. In 2002, when Roger had gone off to Puerto Vallarta for a vacation, Gisele hired a body guard to watch over him. "There are too many thieves and kidnappers in Mexico," she insisted. He dodged the guard the second day he was there and swiftly moved in to the cottage of his old college roommate, Andrew McGee. The 3-bedroom cottage was upscale and expensive, well-decorated and a real *bachelor's pad*. McGee had occupied it for the past two years, basically doing nothing with his days but snorkeling and boating, and then at night, gambling and then ultimately boozing it out with whatever broad he could find and bed down.

The pair caroused for quite a while, drinking, dating, and smoking dope. McGee was the great-grandson of cosmetics tycoon, Harry Montgomery, who began an empire with lipstick and nail polish in the 1930's. He was spoiled rotten, had a peculiar take on life and what he was entitled to, but worse, was into total debauchery when it came to women.

In the end, Roger had no idea how close he came to misfortune with this misguided friendship, for Andrew McGee's nature and motivations were flawed and filled with evil intent. McGee had his own hidden agenda.

In all Roger had stayed at McGee's home in Mexico for three rowdy weeks. He'd finally packed up and left after a shameful incident. The night after a makeshift party, he'd discovered a young woman, cowered and naked and crying hysterically in the bathroom. He helped find her clothing and drove her back to her hotel, and never quite knew what happened. That is – until he read the newspapers a year later – and learned McGee had been arrested and charged with using the so-called "date rape" drug GHB. Evidently Andy dropped something into the girl's drink that night. A sensational trial followed in 2007, with other young women coming forth to lodge charges. McGee, while claiming that the sex had been consensual, was found guilty of 37 charges of raping three different women.

Roger's gradual softening into a Hallmark-style sentimentality started with the McGee episode. He was well aware of how close he came to getting involved in a criminal incident. Now, the morning after his driving with that young lady to the motel, as far as he was concerned, the worst he was guilty of was getting too damned drunk; he had to stop and sleep it off. Or was that all? He hated to admit it, even to himself, but he did grope the lady, had made a total schmuck of himself. Yes, Tessa McMullan – maybe she was even listed in the Manhattan phone book. Roger just couldn't take thoughts of that beautiful blonde out of his head. There was something special about that woman.

Tessa arose from her Yoga position. She had done stretching exercises, and then had meditated for twenty minutes and now had performed ten minutes of movements that helped her feel relaxed. Still her phone had rung so many times during the night – and the few times she awakened to answer it no one spoke on the other end so she took it off the hook. She felt it was Ryan, still not giving up, but there was little else she could do about it. How could she be sure? If it was him, he was definitely stubborn about letting go. How do you get someone to take no for an answer?

The doorman rang the intercom. "There's a delivery, Miss McMullan, looks like a box of flowers. Do you want me to allow the boy up?"

"Yes, that will be fine," she responded. Tessa reached into her wallet and took out two dollar bills to give to the delivery boy.

The door buzzer rang and Tessa, carefully keeping the guard chain on the door opened it. It was a young man with a long white box of some kind of flowers. She was happy to see something positive coming her way. She opened the door, took the box and gave him the tip.

She rushed to open the box, wondering who it was from. "Oh this is hideous," she cried out. The box was filled with black flowers, dyed black flowers, in various stages of decay. And no note. What florist shop was it from? Suddenly Tessa realized the box was not marked. And worse, that she opened the door to someone who wasn't really a delivery boy at all. Just a courier with a very dark message. She was frightened. This was getting to be serious. Maybe she should ask Katy for help?

It is important to our friends to believe that we are unreservedly frank with them, and important to friendship that we are not.

— MIGNON MCLAUGHLIN

CHAPTER FIVE

"You're going to love him, kiddo," Tessa promised, applying a coat of hot pink nail polish to her toenails while juggling the phone.

"Did you tell him—well—that I'm a little overweight?" Angel asked.

"Oh, yeah. Sure. 'Hey, Brendan, I'd like you to meet my fat friend. She's not really *obese* and anyway, she packs her own block and tackle.'

Had Angel eaten an extra bowl of stupid that morning? Who would tell a prospective date he was going to meet Ms Sumo Universe?

"Hell, don't worry about it, Angel. Brendan is a nice guy but he's kind of shy. He's from a good family. He hasn't passed the NY Bar yet but my dad has him working in his law firm.

"Really? Well, knowing your father, he has to have real potential or your dad wouldn't have hired him."

"Oh yes, daddy is very demanding."

"That's why he's so successful. What does Brendan look like?"

"Well, to tell the truth, Angel, Brad Pitt has nothing to worry about. But he's a good catch! So with your gorgeous face, hon, what do you have to lose? I mean, just wear something black and tell him to meet you at Il Tonnello's. It's dark as hell in there!"

Ouch! Wear something black and meet in the dark. Just her face glowing in the gloom like the ethereal smile on the chops of the Cheshire cat. Heaven forbid he was to see the rest of her!

But that was Tessa, never did edit before she spoke. And Angel put up with it.

"Well, gee, okay, Tessa. When he calls, I'll say yes. And thanks. Thanks for thinking of me."

"Please, dear Angel; what are friends for?"

Tessa congratulated herself. Her mother had suggested that *she* should go out with this doofus. She had stopped by her dad's law firm, taken one glance at Brendan Mahoney and known immediately that this was a no-brainer. He wasn't for her; much too nerdy. Foist him off on Angel. Who knew? Maybe the two of them might actually like each another! And anyway, thought Tessa, Angel had to get out more often, so she was doing her a good turn. Sometimes, just by going out, you opened other doors, she rationalized.

Three days later, make that evening, Angel Manelli, dressed to the nines in a new Anne Klein black silk dress, sat at the bar at Il Tonello's. Sat waiting patiently for Brendan Mahoney.

In the mirror behind the bar she saw a narrow-shouldered man in an ill-fitting suit approaching her. "God almighty," she thought, "this geek better not be him."

The 'geek' was around 5'8" short. His complexion was a mottled: red in places and leper–white in others. His hands were like a woman's—soft with fat fingers. Yuck, was this the man Tessa thought she'd like?

It was.

Two hours crept at the pace of a crippled snail. Two hours of mind-numbing conversation about copyright laws and trademarks. She signalled for a second basket of bread. She sent the blood from her brain to her stomach with a third bowl of pasta. She followed the pasta with Tiramisu. She knew that when she got home she would open a quart of Haagen-Dazs cherry vanilla and wolf it all. She craved sweetness. She needed some sweetness in her life.

"Hey this was fun. Want to do it again?"

Brendan smiled and Angel noticed a small spinach leaf stuck between his front teeth. She lowered her gaze and saw that his fly was open. Had it been that way all evening, or did it happen when he went to the men's room?

"Help! Let me out of this nightmare!" It was a silent scream. Tessa. Damn! She should have known better.

"So, want to do this again?" he repeated.

"Let me think about it, Brendan."

"Take your time."

"I've thought about it. No. Sorry. Just don't think we're a match."

Angel didn't want to hurt his feelings but no, no, *no!* He was all wrong.

"Uh huh. Well, hey, can't win 'em all!"

O would some Power the gift to give us, thought Angel, *to see ourselves as others see us!* She wondered what Brendan actually saw in the mirror when he shaved.

She shook his hand. It was limp and clammy.

Phooey. Just another bad blind date in a long string of family-and-friend fix-ups.

Chalk it up to another wasted night. How could Tessa think she'd find Brendan interesting? Angel wasn't that naïve. Tessa was dumping someone on her. Not nice. Not nice at all.

Take off clothes. Hang up clothes. Remove makeup. Waddle to refrigerator. Open freezer. Boy, did that ice cream taste good!

But even a quart of cherry vanilla couldn't fill the emptiness inside Angel. She went to bed with her vibrator.

Angel arrived at the office of *American Beauty Magazine* at her usually punctual 9 a.m. The hours were 9.30 to 5.30, but she learned long ago that to make a good impression one should always be early. She liked to get there before most of the staff, hoping that someday Roger Farnsworth, the publisher, would notice how hard she worked. She fantasized his telling his managing editor, Amanda Kelly, that Kelly should seriously consider promoting Angel. And in Angel's dream she was made an editor.

It was two years since Angel had been hired to work in the fashion department of the magazine, mostly helping the fashion editor in putting together spreads and assisting at the photo shoots. But the work didn't afford her any opportunity to use her creativity. Angel knew she could write good copy and be a first-class editor, if only someone would give her a chance.

And most crushing was that Angel saw other women who had begun in the magazine's training department as she had, move up the ladder, yet she was still just an assistant to the editor. She wondered if it was because of her weight, that she didn't look as put together, as sharp as the others at the magazine. Her weight was always an issue. She tried Weight Watcher's, Jennie Craig, the South Beach Diet, the Atkin's Diet, and two stays at the Canyon Ranch to exercise and lose pounds. She lost some, but it just didn't stay off.

"Angel, did you order the Michael Kor's shoes for tomorrow's shoot?" Kimberly Woodside, the fashion stylist, asked.

"I ordered them in the size 9 the model will wear and I also ordered a 10; they say they're a tight fit."

"Good enough. Here, take this stack of papers and run off copies for me, please," Kimberly directed.

Damn! What a waste. Why did she get these dumb jobs, using the photo copy machine, ordering accessories? Why couldn't she get to write the captions at least? Why wouldn't anyone give her a chance? Angel bit her lip and took the papers over to copy. She had to get promoted soon, she just had to.

"Cara Mia Mine," was one of the many romantic Italian ballads that Carmine Manelli, Angel's father, would sing to her. He loved them all—Perry Como, Dean Martin, Johnny Roselli, Vic Damone—all the old-time Italian crooners. He played the music loud and clear in the sound system of his Blue Moon Yacht Company on City Island in New York, not that far away from the family home in Westchester.

Angel's three older brothers, Mario, Anthony and Carmine Jr. were active in the boat company (which did more than 3 million in sales each year) and her father gave her an easy-enough office job in the firm so she could go to a local junior college and work part time. Carmine doted on his only daughter.

What he didn't know was that Angel wasn't particularly happy with him, or rather, his behavior. Working at the family business it didn't take long for Angel to realize that her father was spending all those extra 'work-related' hours with the company bookkeeper. Fifteen years on, Roseanne Corado was still working at the company and earning more like a CPA's salary than that of a simple bookkeeper.

It offended Angel when she discovered that her father was having an extra marital affair. And as hard as it was to admit, Roseanne wasn't the first one. Damn it, Angel's dad regularly cheated on her mother. Lorraine Manelli was a good mother and a good wife and Angel suspected, probably knew her husband's many late nights were not all due to taking clients out to business dinners.

Also, her brothers worked there; they had to know. And they obviously didn't care. After all, they were young Italian studs, doing their own thing.

It pained Angel to see the looks between Roseanne and her father, the times she noticed him stroking her arm. And it made her feel stupid to think he didn't think she was sharp enough to notice. Yet what could she do but bite her tongue and keep her feelings to herself? And eat another donut or two. Angel learned she could swallow her feelings along with food.

She shared her unease with her brother, Tony. "Hey Angel," he said, "Calm down. So dad has a mistress? He's careful; keeps mom happy. He's always worked damn hard to support our family, to give each of us the best of everything. Leave him alone."

"Oh damn it, Tony," she spat. "You're just like the rest of them; led around by your penis like it's a metal detector. For God's sake, you're going to be 35 next week and you still have no desire to settle down. Why don't you try practicing random acts of intelligence and conscious acts of self-control?"

She stormed out slamming the door behind her.

Something had to change. She couldn't share what she had learned with her mother; there was too much chance of hurting her. And she was getting absolutely nowhere working in the family business. Angel was a bright and fun person. But she felt like she was stuck, neither growing nor getting where she wanted to be. Her family was old-fashioned in some ways, very Italian old-school. They didn't believe in therapy, but she was going to ask her parish priest for a recommendation; someone to see, a counselor at least, because she knew there was more to life than this, that she deserved better. Hell, she wanted a happy ending.

And she'd do whatever was necessary to achieve it.

It Could Be that the Purpose of Your Life is Only to Serve as a Warning to Others.

....

CHAPTER SIX

Languishing at home in their soaring tower in the sky, Vera gazed out the window to the street scene far below her. The sounds of the city could be heard all around. Cabs and cars whizzed along while somewhere a gloved doorman whistled loudly for a taxi. Manhattan was a marvelous city – probably the best one in the entire world. She was proud to own just a little part of it. The co-op apartment was situated on the 19th floor and, oh, were there glorious views.

Yet while she should be feeling content, right now she felt discouraged and empty.

Vera slid further down the dark hole, deep into a numbing defenseless-ness. What was wrong with her life? In spite of everything, there was nothing. All the while she sat there she could hear the newly installed surround sound system playing one of her favorite selections: *"Down in the Depths on the 90th Floor,"* an ancient Cole Porter tune. She adored listening to songs with a sinuous, brooding quality, tunes with a blue note that echoed her ennui. Right now Mabel Mercer was singing the Porter lyrics – a lament to lost love and the perils of excess. *"I'm deserted and depressed in my regal eagles nest, down in the depths on the 90th floor."* Yes, it definitely matched her poor-me mood.

Vera had confided in Tessa, about her marriage, about her general boredom and not knowing what to do with her days. To Tessa's way of thinking what was missing from Vera's life was some good sex and more of it.

"Therapy is expensive. Popping bubble wrap is cheap. And having an affair is even better. You choose," she suggested.

"I don't know if I have the guts to do it."

"Listen, you have a right to a healthy sex life, and if Jason isn't doing it for you, maybe you should take a look out there in the universe."

"I don't think cheating is the answer."

"Hey, sitting alone far too many days and nights, not feeling satisfied, and his not understanding your needs, that isn't the answer either."

"I've tried. Tried for years to get Jason's attention. He's at work too damned many hours – schedules surgery after surgery – I don't think he'd even notice if I disappeared for a few days," Vera remarked, her contemptuousness barely hidden. She was disgusted with her marriage, with her entire life. Damn it. She hated to admit if but so many philosophies and religions espoused the tenet that money didn't buy happiness. Was that just to keep the poor contended with their lot? Or was the wealth and security, all the material benefits she now possessed, meaningless without love?

Naah!! Don't tell me this is it. That even with our beautiful Park Avenue apartment, all the expensive designer clothing I own, more important, the time to pick and choose what I want to do, that whatever I thought would bring me happiness doesn't seem to mean a damn? There has to be more, she sighed. Vera's mind was racing round in meaningless circles. What good was money and social position without a sense of purpose, without someone to share all of this with? Furthermore, the sex between them was never very good, and Vera who was stunningly fit, needed sexual satisfaction. She was starving inside. If not for love, at least for physical contact, affection, ecstasy. Maybe Tessa was right.

That Wednesday morning Vera sat down at her new lap top, (purchased specifically for this campaign; she couldn't afford to have Jason trace any activities on their home computer) and eagerly went on line to explore the personal ad sites. Finally, something that kindled her interest! She avoided the Catholic one, the Christian one, even the Jewish one, rejected the over 40 singles site and decided to go with Match.com, quickly establishing her own specifications for an *"s or d w m"* (single or divorced white male). She'd decide later if age or looks mattered when she read the rest of each man's description. Soon enough, she and Tessa, (who gleefully joined her later that afternoon), were poring through dozens of allegedly eligible men who might make for interesting *assignations*; because, frankly, at this point – a tryst was all she was really seeking.

"Now who wants to go out with someone who admits to having a first name like Herman? Oh no, Herman, you're not my type," Vera laughed, studying the description and picture of a slightly balding man who looked like he was approaching 50. "Who cares if he's a lawyer, I mean can you believe it? Have you noticed that there seem to be dozens and dozens of lawyers looking for love on line?"

"They have even less time to get out there in the "*meat market*", all those long work hours," Tessa suggested.

"Yucch, Tessa, look at that schnozzola on his face!" Vera said, dismissing this Herman candidate speedily.

"It doesn't bode well for an *Australian Kiss*" Tessa sniggered.

"What on earth is that?" Vera asked.

"A kiss down under, darling!

They both giggled.

Scrolling through another dozen contenders, and finding none to her liking, Vera felt let down. She really thought the process would be easier, but then she was always very picky. "Who was it that said that *all indicators show that the human race is selectively breeding itself for stupidity?* There are an awful lot of stupids out there," Vera commented. "I can't handle stupid. Want some espresso?" she asked.

"But of course, darling, I had a really late night and," yawning and stretching at the same time, Tessa continued, "a double cup of espresso would be nice."

Vera hurried to the kitchen, turned on the espresso maker, quickly brewed up some fresh café oh le, spiked hers with some brandy and handed Tessa the straight one.

"Well la de frickin' da," Tessa giggled. Look at this one. Nice pecs, great face, but look at what he says, Vera: this guy wants someone *"who is independently wealthy"* – obviously he's got his own covert agenda going there!"

"He's looking for a *Sugar Mommy,"* Vera proclaimed, "hell, move on to the next one sweetie."

"Come to think of it, Vera, you may have been *magna cum lauded,* but you better have your smarts on here. There are plenty of con artists prowling around these personals looking for their next victims," Tessa warned.

Still she was quietly wondering if perhaps she should try a little dabbling through the want ads herself. They were want ads, really, men and women <u>wanting</u> to meet and to find –now – what were it they were seeking? Certainly some of them were seasoned personal ad placers who learned this could be an expeditious way to meet and bed down a partner. But others – it seemed they were searching for more. A few of the men were real hunks, and, if they were telling the truth, there were quite a few professionals in the group. Maybe there'd even be a jewel, a real Prince among them? Hhmm, Tessa made a mental note to try this herself some time. But now to helping dear Vera who, in Tessa's opinion, had married a real nerd so no wonder she was miserable. Doctor, Schmoctor, Jason Klinghower was the kind of doofus they all avoided in school.

It would take a week of searching and writing cryptic notes back and forth before Vera had found two men that sounded interesting. One was open about saying he was looking for a romantic partner for candlelight dinners, champagne and love. That sounded like a possible sexual liaison to her. Of course, in this day of AIDS, there would be no sex without first knowing more about the person, possibly requesting a recent medical report, never mind protection, <u>always</u> protection. Nothing was easy, was it? Looking for love these days was like walking through a war zone riddled with mines. But looking for love was what she was after. Let the games begin.

Friday afternoon, at the Murray Hill Outdoor Café on East 37th Street, Vera sat down and waited for her prospective date. All she knew was his name was Dennis Farber, who claimed to be a dentist, and wrote that he was divorced. Like far too many of the men advertising there was no photo available. But so what. She had done the same. Vera had placed a bouquet of roses where an image would have appeared. She let out a big sigh. She was nervous. Oh well, soon enough, she'd see who this Dennis character was, and see for herself if he looked more like the deformed bell ringer, Quasimodo, or would she luck out and get herself a George Clooney look-alike?

Vera opened her gold Chanel compact to check her makeup. Deciding that she did look first-rate, she applied a wand of gloss to her already glistening lips. The better to kiss you with, my dear, she laughed to herself. She loved this new adventure – this was exciting stuff!

Just so she'd look studious, (and a little bit "racy,") Vera kept the book, with the almost unpronounceable title on the table beside her, the requisite long stemmed red rose on top. She was getting a little edgy and looked at her watch. It was five after one and he was already late. What if he didn't show up? Maybe they should have exchanged cell phone numbers; all of this was arranged on line. She had last-minute thoughts that this was going to be a real bummer. But she was determined and would wait at least a half hour, just in case he was stuck in traffic somewhere.

Vera informed her prospective collaborator that she'd carry a book on love with her, an easy way for him to recognize her. She didn't bother to tell him the odd title:

"Meaning and content of sexual perversions; A daseinsanalytic approach to the psychopathology of the phenomenon of love" by <u>Medard Boss</u> certainly should be a conversation opener, never mind a tongue twister.

Little did she know she wouldn't need the book to launch a dishy dialogue when the stranger from the dating service appeared. You couldn't make this one up: it was her husband.

They keep saying the right person will come along, I think mine got hit by a truck.

···

CHAPTER SEVEN

Tessa was worried. She wanted to tell Katy about the disturbing calls, the crazy way Ryan had acted when he was high, the malevolent box of flowers, the sense she was being followed – but she also remembered that her sister had warned her not to meet anyone through the Internet. She was embarrassed; too embarrassed to admit she might have been wrong.

She remembered back to the time when she decided to look at the personals on the Internet. It seemed so long ago now. It was a lark; she didn't think it would lead to anything – never mind meeting Ryan Booth and getting so involved. Worse now, she wondered if she had a demented stalker on her hands.

It was six months ago when the whole sordid affair began:

"I admit it, I'm bored and kind of turned off by some of the idiots I've been meeting. It's really no fun getting your hopes up over and over and over again. "

"So go for it, honey, try the Internet," Angel encouraged Tessa. She'd already forgiven Tessa for that dumb blind date.

"Well if I'm careful; don't give out too much information, meet them in a public place, only use my first name...it's doable."

"At least you're in control when you're first looking at who is out there – and they're making themselves available – it's _you_ who makes the first choice." Fancy that, for once Angel was playing adviser. Finally, she had something positive to share. That made her feel good.

"I certainly wouldn't mind having the edge. After all, we still know it's a man's world out there, _Women's Lib_, or not," Tessa theorized. "Yet...I don't know."

"I'm surprised at your hesitancy. You were always such a risk-taker."

"Well, yes and no. Somehow I sense I should be cautious. Then again — Oh hell, I should give it a try! Why should men do all the picking?"

"Yeah, they sure have the upper hand on things, don't they?"

"As a matter of fact, our friend Vera did it recently; was smart enough to use a false identity to avoid any embarrassment.

Angel looked shocked. "Get outta here! She's married, I don't believe this!"

"Vera hasn't been happy for a long time. Jason is all wrapped up in his medical career. And since they never had children...well."

"Gosh...ya never know what's going on behind closed doors. My mom, she's had her problems with dad, but she's got all of us kids. It helps.

"I was over at Vera's. She'd searched the web and signed on to a couple of sites. The men she showed me on Match.com looked normal enough. Of course, she's essentially looking for a one-night stand – at least nothing too complicated – so she has different standards than you or I."

"Puleese – don't tell me she's looking for an affair."

"Shhh, I suppose I shouldn't have said anything. I don't even know what happened; if she followed through or not. She's been kind of mum about things lately, not like Vera. I think I'll pin her down, find out more."

"Whatever. So how about it? Why should she be the only one with some courage?"

Tessa was tantalized.

"Seek and Ye Shall Find," Angel coaxed.

"Okay, you've convinced me to at least take a look."

"So come over to my place this evening. I've done a little search of my own. I'll show you all the sites that are for younger women. Women with real class and quality, of course. Maybe you can find someone who is in your league. I mean, what do you have to lose? Besides, it will be fun."

"One of the first sections I read is the weddings and vows in the Sunday Times. As a matter of fact, I've read of marriages in the NY Times where the couple met through online dating, I mean the New York Times. Now, there's your real stamp of approval."

"Good enough; I'll stop on my way home from the office and pick up some Chinese food. Can you be there by seven?"

"Done. Just get me a tofu dish, please."

"You got it."

See you later then," Tessa said, hanging up the phone.

Angel had met a few men at a Catholic Singles Website, and while none were quite the answer to her dreams, Tony Ruggerio, (who looked like a carbon copy of Al Pacino), was the best of the lot and really kind of sexy. She'd told Tessa and the girls about meeting him. At first the Bod Squad opined that it was risky business to place or answer personal ads. But advertising in the personals had been in the mainstream for years. And Angel could at least provide evidence that at least one of the men she'd met was "dateable" – that he was completely ordinary (maybe too ordinary, but she wouldn't admit to that) and most certainly not a threat.

Angel and Tony dated a few months and that was more than she could say about most of the other guys she'd been meeting in the more conventional manner. Unfortunately, right from the beginning, Angel recognized that Tony wasn't exactly what she would want as a permanent partner – he wasn't husband material.

Tony Ruggerio was satisfied with his high school technical degree, with earning a living as a car mechanic and was content living at home with his family. While he was handsome and was a decent enough guy, he wasn't exactly an intellectual heavyweight. In the four months they kept company, he never wanted to go to the theater nor any of the movies Angel enjoyed, and although it was a relief that he never objected to her being overweight (his mother was a heavyweight herself) Angel soon grew tired of him. Besides, she'd like to live up to her own higher thoughts of herself and Tony, he was willing to settle for less. Less is not what Angel was all about.

After working out at the gym for an hour, Tessa called her modeling service to see if there were any jobs. Nothing. She purchased the local *Show Business* weekly to see if any open auditions were happening. Again, nothing for which she'd be suitable; no soaps, no ingénue roles. Zilch. Oh well, she'd do the best she could with the rest of her day. At least tonight she'd have some fun at Angel's apartment.

In the end Tessa was enthusiastic about looking for a man via the Internet and saw it as an adventure. Why not! Hell, she absolutely adored the movie, "*You've Got Mail,*" and besides that, what was there to lose? After the debacle with Roger Swanson, and then almost a repeat scene with Chase Ekstrom, the wannabe actor who she picked up at the last celebrity party (boy did he tie one on!) Tessa was discouraged.

But not for long. Tessa prided herself on being a gambler in the romance area. And so there she was, later that Tuesday evening in September, sitting side by side at the computer with Angel – looking at a whole world of possibilities. Tessa, eyes wide open, was studying the pictures and brief bios of an assemblage of appealing and appalling men – professionals, low brows, high brows, some brawny types with six pack abs displayed in shirtless photos, and definitely a few in the flock that really peaked her interest.

Enoch Butler, Taylor Meece, Rob Rosen, Ryan Booth. She printed out all of their ads. Each seemed to have the right qualifications – that is, if they were really who they said they were. She would soon find out.

Darn it! Most of the men she'd spent hours selecting on the singles site turned out to be far-flung illustrations of how they'd described themselves. For instance, she'd gladly met up with Enoch at the Regency Bar for a drink…he was alright, but damned if she didn't think he was a little swishy. And when she saw him making eyes at the bartender, and passing him his calling card as he left the tip, she knew she was right. No, definitely not her type.

Then there was Taylor Meece, a corporate attorney, who set up three different appointments with her and had to cancel each and every one of them because he always ended up *getting tied up at meetings with clients.* Who the hell wanted someone like that? Busy, busy, always busy with work. It reminded Tessa too much of her father.

Next misadventure: Rob Rosen. Now there was a real loser. He was the one with the great body and even greater smile. When they spoke he said he was "in real estate" and that he was 32. What he failed to mention was that he was the superintendent of a building in the West Village, was at least ten years older than he said he was (yes, men did lie about their age) and looked like he could use a bath. True, he was a budding author, working on the great American novel, but he didn't have a penny to spend on dinner, his nails were dirty, and Tessa couldn't wait to say good night.

And then there was Ryan Booth, and yes, he seemed interesting. Thirty-five, never married, the co-owner of "BLAST!" the new hot disco on West 48th Street, he was always so busy working, that on a dare, he had put his picture up on the singles site, to see if he could meet a decent and not totally crazed babe. Ryan was both surprised and pleased when a dazzling young blonde like Tessa responded.

Tessa liked what she saw, too. Ryan was a very handsome six footer, with a swagger to his walk and an obvious confidence. He drove the right car (a

Porsche), wore the right watch (a Cartier) and looked great in an Armani jacket over jeans. He took her to dinner the first night, didn't even bother to take her back to his club. "I'll call you tomorrow, sweetheart," he said. "I have a party going on tonight that I have to take care of, I know you won't mind," he added with a twinkle and charm that seemed very convincing. Tessa was pleased, excited, thought there was something in this for her.

What Tessa didn't know was that Ryan was an habitual coke user, and unsurprisingly most of the time it affected his reasoning abilities. Never mind his emotional balance. To the few who knew him well, he was known to have a hair trigger temper. Like the time he beat up his girlfriend, Melanie, so bad that he had to pay $10,000 for her to get her teeth capped, and of course to keep her quiet. He didn't like to be played with. With his Irish temper and the designer drugs that enhanced his paranoia, Ryan wasn't one to put up with crap from any broad. He liked Tessa, she was pretty, great figure, yes, and he'd definitely call her. Just as soon as he could finish with business that night, and catch up on some sleep later.

"So what. So I'm succumbing to the bottom-line mentality of the single woman – and looking for love in all the wrong and right places," Tessa defended her position.

"But you're a beautiful young woman, bright, have many great qualities, and well – I just hope you'll be careful," Katy warned. "Like don't give them your home address; use your cell phone so they can't trace you back to where you live and always meet in a public place at first."

"Well, I'm flattered that you care, sis. And I'll be careful. I've had my share of crazies out there – believe me, I know.

Nice of Katy to show that she was concerned; Tessa appreciated this. She'd told her older sister all about her latest adventure and of meeting Ryan. She was surprised that Katy seemed so cautious. But then, Katy saw the worst in human behavior and wasn't as trusting about men, about anyone.

Too bad Tessa didn't heed her sister's warning. Little did she know it, but she would get herself involved with a real head case, a nasty son-of-a-bitch who didn't like being rejected. Eventually Ryan Booth would become very dangerous to our leading lady, very dangerous indeed.

Oh, life is a glorious cycle of song,
A medley of extemporanea;
And love is a thing that can never go wrong;
And I am Marie of Romania.

— DOROTHY PARKER

CHAPTER EIGHT

At first sighting Vera was mortified. She wanted to get up and just run – run far, very far away.

This can't really be happening; it has to be a nightmare. Pinch me, please and I'll gladly wake up.

But the figure across from her, that receding hairline, the metal-rimmed glasses, the oh-so-familiar face, and, the grin from cheek to cheek, (yes, he was smiling!) – There could be no mistake – no, not at all. It was Jason, her husband, the man she'd been planning to deceive.

He'd strolled over unhurriedly without a bit of hesitation. Glancing quickly at the book on the table and the solitary long-stemmed rose atop, (her credentials for the clandestine meeting); he uttered a quick *"May I?"* then pulled out the chair and slickly sat down.

She couldn't run. She couldn't hide. It would be totally inane – after all, she'd have to face the music and her husband eventually. Never mind she was facing him now.

But wait a minute – hold on! – She suddenly realized: If he was sitting opposite her – why then, he was guilty of the same transgression; damned if he wasn't looking for a lover!

Everything stopped like a freeze-frame in a movie: The din of honking horns from street traffic, the dialogue from nearby tables disappeared. Even the clanging of dishes as a bus boy cleared a nearby station – all of it was drowned out by this awkward moment as the two of them seemed frozen in time.

"Hell!" Jason knew what this scene meant; just why Vera was sitting there with that pitiful book on sex and the rather low-cut dress. *Damned if she didn't look good. He'd have to utter something – speak first. After all, he was a gentleman. But what could he say? This was an absolutely grim state of affairs. He felt like a total fool.*

Shit! What kind of story can I make up? Vera considered. *None, none that won't make me look even worse.*

It was at least a full agonizing minute, sixty long seconds – go on, count them – before anyone spoke.

"I'll be the first to admit it – this is – well – almost laughable," Jason said. "Talk about dumb and dumber."

Vera laughed uneasily. Then Jason. What else could they do? It's said that laughter is the shortest distance between two people and at this moment, they needed to bridge the abyss that had brought them to this incredibly embarrassing episode.

And then, yes, at that split second, Vera and Jason dissolved into two people who had to confront a cruel reality – their marriage was in real trouble. By some peculiar quirk of fate, they were at this outdoor café, having assumed false identities and, worse, possessing a rancorous raison d'être for this get-together. Now, sitting at the same table – looking into each other's eyes – they both knew they'd have to muddle through it, all the way to the truth.

"Would you like a drink?" he asked her.

"If I don't have one soon, I think I'll faint," she answered, shakily.

"Me too." He smiled.

Jason waved the waiter over. "Two martinis, dry, please."

"Now you never drink when you're working and you do have to go back to your office, I assume…?"

"Never assume anything, my dear. I have the afternoon off."

She wondered if that meant he thought whoever he was meeting was going to be a quickie, a meet-and-make-love-in-the-afternoon affair? Hell, would he be that reckless? How could he determine if the woman he would meet was sexually responsible, that she didn't have any disease? Doctor, Schmoctor, Vera thought. There's no way he knows what a sexual liaison could bring in the way of social disease!

She bit down on her tongue to keep from lashing out at him. *"I mean when you think about it, this ass hole could have slept with someone who had herpes and then foisted it upon me, the bastard!"* Vera was seething, quietly enraged. But then anger could mask shame, and she was feeling unspeakable remorse at being there. Or was it only at being found out? OMG! What was she feeling? She was confused. Then again, thinking about their failing marriage, how she had suffered long enough from his ignoring her never mind the lackluster love making. Nah. She didn't feel at fault – it was really more embarrassment at being found out.

"Hey, hon., I don't want to sound like a smart Alec quoting the *Man* – Albert Einstein – but Einstein once said that only two things are infinite – the universe and human stupidity. I am certainly guilty of being stupid – so now, don't you feel too bad," he said, placing his hand on top of hers.

"Have you – have you ever done this before?" she asked with trepidation.

"No, no, no, this was my first time…I didn't know what to do…I knew we were in trouble; that you weren't satisfied, I know it sounds crazy Vera," he whispered, "but I wanted to see what someone else thought."

"A seal of approval?" she asked facetiously.

"Whatever."

The drinks arrived. Thank God. Vera didn't hide how she felt as she swallowed most of it in just four swigs. She had to calm her nerves.

"Let's get out of here," he suggested. "We have to talk, but not in this public arena."

"Okay, we could go back to the apartment, talk there?" she suggested.

"Splendid idea."

Jason took out a ten dollar bill, left it on the table, took Vera's arm to guide her through the tables and out to the street where he hailed a taxi.

While she felt shattered and he was thoroughly embarrassed there was a hint of hope in how they both felt at that moment; that maybe this was a good thing – their discovering each other's cry for help. At least, they could talk, and there would be no recriminations. After all, they'd found each other out.

Vera crossed the threshold of the den, ignored the blinking answering machine, and headed straight to the bar. Hell! They could both do with another drink. Jason was right behind her; tossing off his jacket as he entered the room. He'd purchased the Brooks Brothers Tweed with the suede patched elbows to evince a more casual look, but somehow he knew he hadn't pulled it off. Maybe it was the white shirt he wore? Maybe he didn't look that sharp? What the hell was he thinking about? As if how was what really mattered? Jason realized his judgment was way off the chart. How could he really explain putting up that personal ad? He hoped he could handle whatever was next.

Vera walked over to the sound system and turned it on – music to mellow the tension in the air might make this easier. She chose an oldie – Bobby Short singing at the Carlisle – a recording she'd obtained recently after the café society singer had died. She thought his witty versions of most songs would be up tempo enough for this grey afternoon – a point in time where the truth would be exposed, where they'd have to confess to their mutual sins. But instead of one of Short's more upbeat numbers, the first track that played was the tear-jerking *"Every time We Say Goodbye…."* one that usually evoked within her that old fear of abandonment, maybe because her father had died when she was so young.

The Cole Porter lyrics were haunting: *"Every time we say goodbye, I die a little, Every time we say goodbye, I wonder why a little, Why the Gods above me, who must be in the know. Think so little of me, they allow you to go."*

Jason strolled over to her, touched her arm tenderly and said, "Let's dance."

When you're near, there's such an air of spring about it, I can hear a lark somewhere, begin to sing about it., There's no love song finer, but how strange the change from major to minor, Every time we say goodbye.

The song played on. And as they did, long ago feelings of love emerged.

How did things change so suddenly? Where did the passion come from?

They hadn't danced in years and now there they were clinging on to one another and feeling an intimacy they hadn't felt for far too long a time.

After, they sat down quietly, neither of them saying a word.

As they disappeared into the yielding velvet sofa, he touched her leg, then her inner thigh. All of a sudden she felt excited. They were supposed to be talking. But instead they both felt a longing for one another, an impulsive need to be physically close.

Without saying a word Jason picked her up, carried her into the bedroom, and almost ripped off her top in his urgency to touch her breasts, to fondle her all over.

She could feel his erection, hard, strong, and for the first time in maybe forever she wanted to touch it, to let him know that she wasn't afraid of how it felt. She unzipped his pants and rubbed it gently, ever so gently as she heard him breathe even harder.

This was incredible, magical, totally unexpected that the two of them would find themselves in the heat of passion, making amazing love. There was an ardor, an excitement neither had felt before that had them almost whirling, spinning out of control. The sex was good and getting better as he kissed her all over her body and she for the first time in their marriage – she leaned down and kissed him down there – put her tongue there, let him know she wanted him, wanted him badly.

They made love feverishly and it was so good, so really good that Vera came, came even before Jason did. Would wonders never cease?

She turned over, sighed, and said, "We should advertise more often."

"I'll second that," he laughed.

And they both fell asleep.

Dying is easy. Living is hard.

— DOROTHY PARKER

....

CHAPTER NINE

<u>*Story in local New York newspaper, Sept. 2012:*</u>

A Manhattan love doctor has been slapped with malpractice suits for breaking hearts.

Fertility specialist Dr. Zamoor Kharlin, a married father of three, allegedly left a trail of tears after taking to the Internet for some extramarital romance, according to court papers made public yesterday.

Kharlin, 46, is being sued by two women he met through an online dating service - and allegedly wooed with bizarre come-on lines invoking the Devil, tales of past lives and talk of the Apocalypse.

In lawsuits, Tiffany Jordan and Joan Chen, two of the alleged victims, branded him a medical masher who pretended to be single to lure them into sexual relationships.

According to court papers, he may have been sweet-talking as many as six women at or around the same time.

"Kharlin's conduct was part of a larger pattern in which he approaches single women on the Internet and becomes romantically involved with [them]," Jordan, 35, charged in a complaint filed Wednesday in Manhattan Supreme Court.

Kharlin's conduct "was outside the boundaries of human decency and societal norms," according to the lawsuit.

Shit, piss and corruption! His mother's favorite expletive poured out of his mouth like an erupting volcano. Jason Klingenhower, M.D., couldn't believe what he was reading. To think that he'd resorted to using the Internet for meeting women just a few months ago. He didn't know the physician, but just reading the sensational charges was enough. That idiot obviously had a surfeit of chutzpah! Now the doctor was in deep shit!

He'd show it to Vera, but not now; not with her worrying about her mother. Right now she was on her way up to Mercy Hospital in Larchmont to visit her mom, who was still listed in serious condition after suffering a stroke.

Jason had made a professional call, had spoken with the doctor on duty. *Mrs. Stern was in guarded condition, but the doctor felt that she would recover from the stroke.* Tests were to be administered that morning. Jason anticipated driving up that evening to visit his mother-in-law; however he had a surgery an hour from now and had to focus on his work. Anna was such a good lady; he hoped she'd pull through this without any lasting impairment.

Judi McMahon

Lower Manhattan – A few days before…..

"I don't want anyone to know I'm paying for this," Ryan Booth whispered in an ominous tone. They were sitting in his car, just before the entrance to the Lincoln Tunnel, a long enough haul from his Soho loft, to be undetected. He didn't want to use his cell phone, nothing to trace him to this meeting with his brother Evan. Evan really could use some easy money. He had agreed right away to Ryan's plan, which was to exact revenge on some cu*t who had given Ryan a bad time. Good. Evan lived far enough away in Newark, New Jersey to avoid being on any radar screen. Ryan was dogged. This clever little plot was fool-proof. Funny, he really enjoyed creating the plan; developed each detail fastidiously. It was crucial that nothing could be tracked back to him.

Women! Evan had had his fill of them. He could certainly commiserate with Ryan. Evan had paid his dues. Divorced, fathering three kids with two different bimbos – kids that he couldn't support – yet having the damn state garnish his salary whenever he tried to earn an honest living – never mind suffering through a bunch of bad news love affairs. Women. All they did was want and want and demand. He'd had his fill of broads.

"Now you have no compunctions about doing this?" Ryan asked.

"Do I look like a people person?"

Ryan smiled. "Wait, I'm trying to imagine you with a personality."

"Ah, hell Ryan, don't hit below the belt. Neither of us had it that easy, growing up in the Jersey slums. So you made it out a little bit better and faster than me. But I got stuck living there longer with that drunken so-called mother of ours."

Ryan didn't want to acknowledge it, but Evan was right. Their mother, Jeanne Marie, she was in and out of rehab places, had resorted to prostitution most of her life, was a wreck of a woman and never really a mother to either of them.

In fact, neither of the boys knew who their dads were – each one was fathered by a different man – some stranger who more than likely paid for sex. Their young lives were hard, lonely, and poor. And their mother – she was nothing better than a whore. They'd be pushed into the other room, but

57

nothing could keep them from hearing her moan and scream and yell dirty words as some stranger who was in her messy, dirty bed was jumping all over her ass. Christ, could he ever forget the filth, the shame of it all? Ryan despised his mother, hated her for being so cheap, so weak, so selfish. It affected him deeply – women couldn't be trusted.

Growing up, both Ryan and his brother were defenseless – helpless little boys who had to depend upon their mother to keep them clothed and fed. And they didn't always get fed regularly, never mind always wearing thrift store clothing. Life was a series of broken promises and a desolate childhood. Their mother destroyed everything with her self-centered drinking. She was in control of their welfare – and failed miserably – ever guilty of neglect. Ryan hated every minute of it. He could hardly wait to get away, to grow up, and to be able to be in charge of his own life. And he would never forget.

In the end the abuse Ryan suffered by his mother's neglect made him distrust all women; he always doubted their motivations; what they really wanted from him. Sure he became successful, yes he was handsome, and getting a babe into bed was nothing. But to find anyone special, a woman to be by his side and to count on – it didn't come easy to Ryan Booth.

And while he never talked about it, somewhere deep down in his craw Ryan felt that he was being used if a woman wasn't responsive to him at all times; if he wasn't in control. Above all else, Ryan had to be in control. And so that one night when he wanted Tessa to do some coke with him and then engage in some real hot sex damned if the bitch didn't say she wasn't in the mood. Ryan couldn't, wouldn't accept it. So he lost it and slapped her hard across the face. He couldn't believe her reaction. That bitch, Tessa, she'd taken off her shoe and hit him with it, breaking his nose. He was bleeding, and it hurt like hell and she just went flying out of his luxe studio apartment above the night club, running down the stairs and away. What a bitch! She would never get away with it. He'd done so much for her, gave her so many gifts.

The next day a messenger had arrived with a carton filled with everything he had given her of value – all the jewelry – everything. That hurt even more. He had made her his woman. How could she reject him this way? Never mind, she almost ruined his good looks by hitting him with that goddamned shoe. Ryan would never ever forget what she did. He'd get even. The box of black flowers he sent her later on – that was his warning. The *cunt* better look out, he was going to get her.

"You ain't got a thing to worry about, I'll get the job done," Evan assured him.

Agreed. The two brothers made a high five sign before Ryan opened his trunk and retrieved a Gucci leather suitcase. Smiling, he handed Evan a neat portfolio containing $20,000 in untraceable $100 bills. Five thousand dollars was to go to Evan – for his finding the right person – who, for $5,000, would then get in touch with another reprobate – the executor who would do just about anything for $10,000 in cash – and who had no moral reservations about the job at hand – to follow this bad-news-bitch, Tessa McMullan – study her habits – find the right moment when she was alone and then to toss the lye in her face. But there had to be six degrees of separation. Ryan knew he could depend upon his kid brother Evan, who'd recently been released from prison after serving a year for assault. Now on parole; Evan had every reason to be very very careful.

Evan had connections; he knew the brand of bad-assed individuals who had no conscience and needed the hard cash. Ten grand was a big deal for many of them, and taking a life, or injuring someone, hell, they didn't think twice.

Ryan was feeling real good about exacting revenge. And using his brother. Evan owed him. He'd hired the best criminal attorney, got him a plea bargain deal and only a year's jail time when the schmuck could have gotten ten. Yeah, Evan would help him get the dirty deed done. That would teach Tessa to offend him like that. She made him look like a total fool in front of his friends. He wouldn't, couldn't let her get away with it. She almost ruined his face. He'd ruin hers for good. Ryan felt better already. He would never ever look back.

Larchmont Hospital

"Your mother is doing fine, Mrs. Klingenhower, but right now she's down stairs getting a new cat scan," Dr. Feinman, the on-duty resident explained. Harried and sleepless most of the time, but especially now, he wasn't in the mood for an hysterical woman. Yet that was exactly how Vera was acting.

She'd lost her poise, her usual calm. Beside herself with worry and concern, and yes, maybe guilt, as soon as she and Tessa drove into the hospital parking lot, she began to fall apart.

"Oh please, dear Lord, don't let her die, please. She is such a good woman, please save her life," Vera pleaded quietly. She always knew what a wonderful mother she had but she didn't pay enough attention, visit her often enough. *Please, don't let it be too late for me to show my mother how much I love her.* Anna Stern deserved a better life; she worked so hard for both her children. She needn't die so young; Vera could take her traveling, spend more time with her, make her life have more quality and meaning now that she lived all alone.

At that very moment, Vera experienced an epiphany. She wanted to do better herself, to find a purpose to her life, to work in a field that would help people. Maybe social work. She could go back to school and take a Masters program and then work with the aged and infirm. She would show her mother that she had learned from her, that work was good, and that helping people was even better.

Some cause happiness wherever they go; others whenever they go.

— OSCAR WILDE

CHAPTER TEN

"This isn't an office. Its hell with fluorescent lighting," Hannah Cohen, remarked. The office wisecracker, she was like a young version of Joan Cusak (who played the side kick to Melanie Griffin in the movie, *"Working Girl"*). She always had a quip or two with which to amuse her co-workers. More important, Hannah was quick to critique the staid old-fashioned customs of Roger Farnsworth, the publisher of American Beauty Magazine and his equally stuffy editor, Amanda Kelly.

Not a mega second later, the door to the copy room opened and in strode Amanda Kelly. "Hannah, this is horrible. You think this copy can be used? To sell what? *Schmates, maybe! Certainly not any issues of our magazine," Amanda pronounced vociferously, not caring a wit that not only was Angel standing nearby, but so were half the staff. It was awful how she could pick on poor Hannah, who really was a good writer, and not care if she was embarrassing her in front of others

"And the typos – really. Don't ever bring me something you haven't proof-read first. Here, I've made notations on the few ideas and phrases I like and what I don't – take another shot at it, won't you?" Kelly said derisively, tossing the papers back to Hannah, and abruptly walking away. *Schmates. *Yiddish term for rags.*

"Oh well, you know it's going to be a bad day when you stumble out of bed and miss the floor. Mine started that way with the hot water out again in our building. And now Miss Kelly has decided to once again attack my work," Hannah said, trying to appear more indifferent than she was really feeling.

"Don't worry, you're a damned clever writer, you'll get it right," Angel said as she gave Hannah a warm hug.

"Thanks. But isn't she a bitch? A real bitch!"

"Shhh, she'll hear you, please," Angel urged. "Let it go." Angel leaned in and whispered: "Besides, I've heard through the grapevine that she may be leaving, moving on to bigger and better things, believe it or not!"

"Really, now wouldn't we all be blessed?" Patrick Prendergast, the travel editor chimed in. "I've had more than enough of the spoiled Amanda myself. She trashed my last column and nixed a trip I wanted to make to the Great Barrier Reefs. Honestly I wanted to go over her head to the big boss. I was actually drafting a memo when the haughty Miss Kelly marched in – but if you have a clue that she's going to get out of here, well, now, wouldn't that be divine!"

"Well, I don't have official information – rather it's data I've gleaned through the drunken half-conversations overheard at crowded press parties this past month," Angel confessed.

"That'll do. You'd be surprised how much you can learn from inebriated lips," Patrick snickered.

"To hell with her, Hannah. Hey, would you do me a favor? I was asked to write a book review for the Observer. Take a look at it, and tell me if you think it's good. Of course, it's extra work – but hell, with what they're paying me here, I need some free lance income."

"Sure, Pat would love to."

Hannah appreciated Prendergast's confidence in her editing abilities. He was really a super guy, good looking, bright, talented. And unfortunately, for her at least, gay. That old story: too damn many of the handsome ones weren't available.

Hannah walked back to her desk and pored over Patrick's book review. Hooray! What good writing. It was a pleasure to read. Like the sentence, *"despite these grandiose intentions, Sullivan quickly brings the novel down to its human essence."*

It only took a ten minute read; there wasn't a typo and his words were strung together like perfect little pearls of prose. Indeed, Patrick's skillful phrasing articulated the spirit of the author's meaning. "Bravo, Pat. I loved the review, you made me want to read the book, and, of course, the writing was flawless," she reported, as Hannah returned Patrick's draft.

"Thanks, Hannah, I can always depend on you," Prendergast said. "You're an ace." Damn it to hell, he thought, this woman is really such a good person. And juicy looking too. I wish I could think of a decent fellow for her. In fact, he concluded; if he was straight, he'd even entertain an affair with her.

She was pleased to get the compliment. Now if only someone out there would recognize her writing talents. Hannah had always wanted to be a writer. For most of her existence on this earth, since the tender age of five years old, as soon as she could put pencil to paper, she'd written poetry. It was her way to express all the secret feelings she had held inside. Words for her were liberating; ideas meant total independence. Finally, two years ago, she'd written a novel, a story based on her own childhood, which wasn't an easy one. In fact, she would sometimes joke, her family history read like a Jewish version of a Charles Dickens novel.

Hannah grew up on the south side of Philadelphia – a poor neighborhood inhabited more by Italians and Irish than Jews. Her father was a salesman, working mostly on commission. One year he was selling encyclopedias, the next insurance, the last one, sneakers at the local Modell's sports store; he never did well at any of them. Her mother, Gittel Cohen, who Hannah could only dimly recall, was exceptionally pretty. Gittel had done the unthinkable: fed up with her husband not being able to hold down a decent job, wanting a more glamorous life, she ran off with another man – the clarinet player in a local band, who wanted to make it to the jazz clubs in the Big Apple, leaving her poor father, Murray Cohen, with her and her kid brother to raise. Worse, she never ever heard from her mother again. No calls, no birthday cards, no nothing.

It was pathetic. Soon after her mother left them (and never looked back) Murray fell apart, (he was never a strong individual) and was reduced to such a deep depression that he had a nervous breakdown. Before long he was in and out of V.A. hospitals. Fortunately, he was a veteran and had benefits, but he really wasn't competent enough to raise his own children. "I have crossed and recrossed the line between sanity and craziness so many times, I have all but rubbed it out," he'd say, knowing his hold on reality was dangling by a thin thread of hope and deliverance. Murray finally gave up. He didn't want his children living with strangers in the foster care system so he took Hannah and her brother to his mother, who was a poor widow, eking out a small living as a seamstress. Fortunately, Hannah's grandmother took them in. But it wasn't easy.

And ever since then, somewhere deep inside of Hannah, there was an awful void, one where she buried old hurts and heartaches. She couldn't figure out what was so bad about her, what was so unloving, that her own mother would abandon her.

Now, grown up and on her own, Hannah had graduated from Hunter College, a good city college with low tuition, and finally, she was working at a magazine, inventing a life for herself and hoping to become a published author. But the competition was fierce.

Hannah's book was brilliant in its honesty and was well-written, but after sending the manuscript out to over 15 literary agents, and getting that many reject letters, she'd taken a break. She really didn't know what to do, but she knew she wouldn't give up. She'd go back and reread and edit the book some more. She remembered a quote from one of her favorite authors, Anais Nin: "*Life shrinks or expands in proportion to one's courage.*" She was a gutsy woman, she would persevere.

Patrick and Hannah shared one thing in common: writing for each of them was a way to discover what they thought. By creating a narrative they could impose a pattern on the chaos of life. For now, Hannah would be content to merely get a better assignment at the magazine. Being a lowly copywriter there, the pay was bad and the interesting assignments rare. Besides that, promotions rarely happened. All too frequently, new people, with *connections,* would be brought in from outside. There was definitely favoritism practiced at American Beauty Magazine. Usually an Ivy League graduate, who knew someone who knew someone else, would get picked over an employee with lesser credentials for a plum position. Hannah, while a pleasant young woman, with auburn hair and large hazel eyes, just didn't fit the image the magazine preferred to demonstrate to its readers.

Hannah and Angel were in the same maddening situation – neither was appreciated for their talents, nor had much chance of moving ahead at the publication. They'd consoled each other over lunch more than once about the unfairness of being passed over. While women had long ago broken through the glass ceiling and the publishing field was a welcoming one for women, at certain publishing houses there was still an underlying snobbery and caste system.

Frustrating, but there was little that could be done about it. Sitting at the local Starbucks, downing their café lattes, the women compared notes.

"Hell, I am not giving up. And by the way, don't tell a soul, but I've been sending my resume out. I have an appointment next week at an ad agency. I'm bringing my portfolio. Maybe, just maybe I'll get the job and it starts at $35, 000," Hannah reported.

"Terrific! I bet you get it. You have such a clever way with words, and good ideas," Angel said encouragingly. "Just think positive and the better job will come along. And remember, the minute you start talking about what you're going to do if you lose out, you've lost!"

"Good advice, Angel! I'll drink to that," Hannah laughed, raising her café latte.

They were about to get up from the table and get back to the office when Angel looked up and saw her old friend, Danny Bianco, walking by. "Hey Danny, Danny, it's me, Angel," she called to him.

"So it is. Wow, how are you Babes?" he smiled. "What has it been – five or six years since we last saw one another?"

The two were classmates in high school. Danny's family also lived in her hometown of Larchmont; his father was a successful restaurateur, being the owner of the celebrated "Bianco's," the town's most popular Italian eatery. It was such a popular restaurant that many of the residents in the area booked their special parties in the elegant private room on the premises. In fact, Angel's graduation party was held at Bianco's. It might have been the last time she saw Danny – he was one of the many invited to celebrate.

"This is my friend, Hannah," Angel said. "So tell me what are you doing these days?"

"I'm finishing law school at Fordham. This is my last year, as a matter of fact. I just happened to be visiting my sister who works down the block. She asked me to bring her some coffee," he explained. "But wow, I'm glad you stopped me."

"Marie – that was your sister's name, right? Wow, small world!"

"Hey, let me have your phone number. Maybe we can have dinner one night?" Danny suggested, sounding like he meant it.

"Sure. I live downtown in Chelsea. Have my own apartment. I'd love to get together," Angel responded. Could this really be happening, could this really terrific guy, nice-looking too, actually be asking to see her?

She took out one of her business cards from her wallet and handed it to Danny.

"Well, what do you know about that! I live on West 18th Street – we must be neighbors!"

"Five blocks apart. I'm on 23rd Street," she laughed.

"Gotta get this coffee to Marie while it's still hot. I'll call you, girl!"

"Go on, pinch me," she turned to Hannah. "Tell me that really happened."

"Hey, it did and he's really a cute guy."

"He probably didn't notice my weight since I'm sitting down."

"Stop it, Angel. Were you thin and svelte when you knew him?"

"You're right, I wasn't. Well, let's see what happens. Maybe he just wants to renew old times and talk about mutual friends."

"Come on; we better get back to the office. But, Angel, think positive. Say to yourself: *God does not ask about our ability, but our availability,*" Hannah advised. "Please, honey, you're a pretty girl, with lots to offer. Be confident. Remember, all you have to do is expect good things and just show up for life! Be available," she repeated with a smile.

"Now aren't you Miss Mary Sunshine! Hey, I like the sound of it. Why not!" Angel said, giving her friend a big hug.

And it was true. Showing up for life was half the battle. Angel would learn this sooner than she might ever imagine. Good things were going to happen to our damsel in distress.

CHAPTER ELEVEN

"Mama – Please, come – I know you'll like it," Angel urged.

"But Manhattan, it's such a long trip for me, darling," her mother, Lorraine, responded.

"Never mind. It's a Friday night. You can take the train in the afternoon and I'll meet you at Grand Central. We'll eat out and then go to the show. It's a fun musical, Ma, songs from the 60s; you'll know 'em — really great ones like "*My Eyes Adore You*," and "*Sherry.*" It's based on Frankie Valli and *The Four Seasons* – the one-time pop singing group with a lot of great hits. I've gotten us great seats too; third row, center orchestra. You can stay over at my place and Saturday we'll both take the train back home."

"What's the name of the show?" her mother asked, forgetting what Angel had told her just a few moments before.

"*Jersey Boys*. It's been a big hit for a few years now. It's really good. I saw it when it first opened. I was lucky to get seats then. And I'm telling you, Ma, you'll enjoy it. You need to get out more often and this should be your new start in life."

"Well, alright my darling daughter. It's really a nice birthday gift."

"And a special one. You're going to reach a special number in a couple of weeks," Angel said, not wanting to pronounce out loud the big number 50.

"Yeahh, time marches on."

"You're still young, Mama," Angel said, overlooking the fact that her mother had seemed to age too much in the past few years. She didn't really take good care of herself; let her hair turn grey, dressed kind of dowdily. Most fifty year old women looked 40 these days. Angel adored her mother; a really good and loving woman, Lorraine Manelli, took better care of her children, her husband and even their home, before considering herself.

"So we'll celebrate at a nice restaurant and then go to the theater. It's my treat for you. I'm really happy you're going to come with me."

"Then this coming Friday, what time should I be there?"

"I checked the train schedule. If you take the express in from Larchmont at 4 p.m. you'll be at the terminal at 5:15. I'll meet you by the big clock, right in the main lobby – I'll get there ahead of time and I'll wait." Angel had already asked to leave work early that Friday to make sure she'd be on time.

"Okay, I'll be there. And I'll bring my little overnight case; we'll have a real mother daughter time of it."

Angel was glad she'd convinced her mother to come into town. Lorraine Manelli rarely did anything out of the ordinary, hadn't even seen a first-run movie in years. A real homebody, she enjoyed watching daytime TV shows like *The Price is Right* and rarely missed a day's viewing of *All My Children* and *As the World Turns*, two of her favorite soap operas.

A dutiful Catholic, Lorraine went to Mass every morning at St. Joseph's, the local church, and then spent a good deal of her day cooking and baking, even though her superior culinary skills were rarely needed these days.

It was that time in a woman's life when the nest was almost empty. This was especially difficult for Lorraine. Tending to her family, feeling needed, this was what she cherished most of all. Now, with her three sons all grown up, and Angel living on her own, there wasn't much for her to do. Never mind her husband, Carmine. He'd always worked long hours, and some nights, he played poker with his friends. The few nights he was home in time for supper, he was rapidly glued to the TV watching Monday night football – or depending on the season – the latest baseball or basketball game. And the boys, while none of them had so far married, and all three still lived at home – they were hardly there.

It saddened Lorraine, but what could she do? This was her life; she didn't feel much needed. With the exception of the obligatory duties of bringing in the boys' shirts to the local laundry and taking care of the dry cleaning for all the men of the house, there was little required of her.

Oh well, at least Carmine earned a very good living with the boat business so they could afford such a beautiful home, and everyone, thank you, Jesus, Mary and Joseph, was healthy. But still it was troubling – with her own parents long gone, and her sister Marie living in Rhode Island with her family – there was little kith and kin, not much of the good old fashioned days when Lorraine felt needed and wanted. Never mind her only daughter, Angel, deciding two years ago that she had to move into the city. Lorraine relentlessly worried about Angel, her overweight problem – her not meeting a decent man. By now she should have married and begun her own family.

Lorraine wasn't dim-witted. Pop psychology shows like *Dr. Phil* and *Oprah* had provided her with some insights. She recognized that she was on the fast track to nowhere; that she needed to do more with her life. She'd spent far too much time taking care of the family and not enough making friends, nor developing her own interests. Finally, that past winter Lorraine decided to volunteer and began helping run the gift shop at the hospital three days a week; that got her out a little. But still, it wasn't enough.

She took out the pasta machine. If she was gone on Friday and Saturday, maybe she could make some lasagna for the boys. She'd make two big pans full, and leave it for them to eat. Besides – Carmine – she knew lasagna was his favorite meal. Such was her life and worse, the family only enjoyed her home cooking sporadically. This one or that one – each was busy with his own interests – dating, sports, whatever. The only time she could rely on them all to spend some quality family time was on Sundays; then all of them, they did sit down to a traditional Sunday afternoon meal. At least she had Sundays.

Taking out the large pots and pans in her kitchen, the fresh tomatoes she'd picked from the garden, the newly picked basil too – all the good ingredients to make her family a delicious meal – Lorraine smiled. Aahh, how she loved her children and Carmine.

The applause was deafening. The audience loved the old songs. And Lorraine Manelli, all dolled up in a lovely maroon colored velvet dress she found in the back of her closet, she looked really pretty.

"This is terrific," she commented to her daughter, as they got up during intermission. How did you know that I'd love the old music? You picked a really good one, honey."

"Come, we can get a glass of wine," Angel suggested, taking her mother's arm.

They walked up the aisle from their center orchestra seats for the 15-minute break. Angel was really feeling super-duper – She was proud of herself, that she was able to treat her mother to a night out like this.

And that's when she saw him, and her, out of the corner of her eye. In the next aisle, walking towards the bar located in the lobby was her father, Carmine. And he wasn't alone. He was holding the hand of his long-time mistress, Roseanne Corado. Roseanne, decked to the nines in a pair of obviously pricey dangling diamond earrings, a glitzy (and very low cut) red taffeta dress, looked damned good for a 40-something ho – yes, that's how Angel saw her – nothing better than a high priced whore.

Worse, Lorraine saw them too. She was looking at the tall attractive woman she knew for years as the office bookkeeper holding hands, walking with her husband. She was shocked, disoriented – no, no – she didn't want to believe what her eyes were seeing. Tears misted over her eyes, blurring the view, as the couple, drinks now in hand, walked out of the lobby to the street where smokers milled about. Lorraine was furious. How embarrassing. And that bitch, Roseanne, besides being a home wrecker – she also smoked her brains out.

"Mom, come on, let's get out of here, please," Angel entreated her mother who looked crestfallen.

"No, I will NOT leave. We will NOT leave. They should. Besides they didn't see us, did they? Your father, he's an adulterer. The man will burn in hell, I tell you," she said, trembling, so obviously upset that Angel helped her mother walk over to the settee in the lobby.

"Please, sit down. I'll get you some water."

Oh Mary, mother of God, help me through this, Lorraine prayed silently. Now lost in the metaphor of her biblical teachings, Lorraine Manelli, devoted, faithful wife of Carmine Manelli for the past 33 years, was devastated as she struggled to hide her shame. Then it came to her – the seventh Commandment – "Thou Shalt Not Commit Adultery." But he had, he was a liar, an adulterer, a thief of all her dreams.

The warning buzzer sounded for the second act. "Come mother, you're right – why should we leave? We will see it through," Angel said, guiding Lorraine back to their seats. She admired her mother for not wanting to leave, that as distressed as she was, she wanted to stay, even if it meant an actual encounter with the culpable couple before they all left the theater. For, while they were seated on opposite sides of the aisle, they were all seated in the orchestra. And, in point of fact, Angel was furious enough to want to run straight into them, to let her father know that he was found out. Damn it, he should have taken his wife for her birthday to see this show, not that floozy from the office!

They sat there through the second act, tried to enjoy the performances, but there were neither more smiles nor joy at the musical performances for Angel or her mother. Still they stayed. Waited it out. And at the end, the music coming to a glorious crescendo, got up with the rest of the audience to give a standing round of applause for the wonderful cast of performers.

"Here, let's take that exit," Angel suggested, pointing to the side door. A face-to-face meeting was futile. There was no point in embarrassing her mother any longer. She had a plan: she'd call her brothers, talk to them, would confront her father later, without her mother having to go through angst and anguish. Right now she wanted to calm her mother down. She'd be with her all through the night and morning, and would console her. Oh my God, if only ice cream were enough. This time she knew it wouldn't make a bit of difference. Something sweet couldn't obliterate the bitterness, the agony of what they'd discovered. The morally wrong betrayal by Carmine of his devoted wife.

"Taxi, here," Angel called, and then helped Lorraine in first. Thank God they were out of there. What a dreadful turn of events this cruel and hurtful birthday present for her mother.

In fact, while Angel never bothered to attend church, she made up her mind to get up early enough to take her mother over to St. Francis for the morning mass. She knew this would be soothing and healing. For her, as well as her mom.

Damn it, was it really true that a faithful husband was part of an endangered species? Her father wasn't the sharpest tool in the shed, but he'd built up a successful boating business and been a generous provider for his family. He'd built her mother a mansion of a home. He still supported Angel, paying the rent on her apartment each month so that the small salary she made would be sufficient. Why, why did he have to turn out to be such a rotten husband? Worse, Angel had suspected the office affair for years; but why did her mother have to find out? This was the greatest sting of all.

"From birth to 18 a girl needs good parents. From 18 to 35, she needs good looks. From 35 to 55, good personality. From 55 on, she needs good cash. I'm saving my money."

— SOPHIE TUCKER

CHAPTER TWELVE

The hang-ups on her home phone were increasingly eerie. She bought a throw away cell job and gave the number to a limited few. Even more creepy, Tessa had a feeling she was being watched. How on earth did she get into this spine-chilling state of affairs? This was getting to be like a bad news segment on *Law and Order*. Finally, afraid to be alone at night, Tessa called on Angel, who was beginning to realize that Tessa was vulnerable and rightfully frightened. She felt responsible, having urged Tessa to take a chance on the personals websites. How could she help? Angel invited Tessa to stay at her place, and so for the next week Tessa took to staying on the sofa at Angel's. But how long could this go on?

"You have to call the police," Angel urged. "Don't wait any longer; it could be some sicko is stalking you."

"I'm pretty sure I know who it is, and I think it's a control issue."

"Control, schlamol! Please, Tessa, we live in a way-out world with its share of weirdos. Not to mention — you have a sister who damn well could help you. Why don't you call her? This waiting game is unwise. You have to be more proactive. As much as I love you and your company, just how long are you going to camp out here? Whoever is mad as hell at you, he'll find out where you are. This is dangerous."

"I, I…really don't want to call Katy."

"Gosh are you stubborn."

It's got to be Ryan…he doesn't like to take no for an answer…and I just didn't want to be with him any longer. He's popular, runs his own club, sure. But once I got to know him better I saw another side of him. He's wired up with coke and that's not for me.

"Well, if it's him, a visit from the police might be a good thing. He wouldn't want to get into any situation where he'd lose his liquor license or get any kind of bad publicity."

"You've got a point there. But I also think this might put him over the edge."

"Hey, Tessa," Angel had another idea. "Remember the Victoria's Secret ad you did? Maybe it's just a freaking delivery person who recognizes that's you looking so sexy. Or how about a weirdo you might have met at one of the many cocktail parties you go to – maybe he saw it and developed his own demented delusions. You can't be sure about anything when it comes to sick and crazy people."

"Look, from what's been happening – I'm fairly sure that it's the night club owner, Ryan Booth. I'm hoping he'll find a new play toy soon. He's just pissed that I wouldn't play his games. Ryan doesn't know how to take no for an answer. I'm fairly sure it's him, I can't think of anyone else who would have any reason to be even slightly annoyed with me, hon. It's not like I go around making enemies."

"It's not a question of your even assuming the tiniest of blame in this matter. More than likely, it has very little to do with you. There are creepy people out there, too many in this universe. And some men, if they were abused by a drunken father or more likely, got bad mothering, develop a secret hate of women. My God, I've been a faithful reader of true crime books for so long, I have no doubt that there are people – no, correction – make that *men* – who for no rational reason, are haters, beasts, evil doers – who will stop at nothing to seek revenge, get their way, maim and kill. It rarely has anything to do with the victims. These people, the BTK killer, Ted Bundy, all of them – they want to control through destroying – and you just might be dealing with a twisted character out there," Angel warned.

"Okay, I'm supposed to go to my parents' this weekend. It's their 35th Anniversary and they're having a party – you know how my mother just loves doing parties. She's been planning this for months now. I'll take Katy aside and ask her for advice."

"Call her, why don't you?"

"Look she knows about this. Well, at least she knows I was putting an ad on the Internet and she warned me even then to be careful."

"Say, could it be any of those other men?"

"Nahh – there was nothing intense in any of those meetings. Only with Ryan did things get out of hand."

"Okay, Tessa. Have it your way. But be careful…."

"Sure. But I do have a photo shoot tomorrow. I've got to go back to my apartment now and get ready. I also have a hair appointment later today. Don't worry, Angel, I'm not even walking around these days. I call car service and go right into a cab. I'm not stupid, you know."

"Here, take this book," Angel said, removing a soft cover copy from her book case. "It's by one of my favorite crime authors, Ann Rule – she was once a police officer and she's been covering true crime cases for years. They're usually about manipulative people. This one, *"If You Really Loved Me,"* is a whopper! The evil one here, he gets others to murder for him, and he even tries to lay the blame on his daughter. Read it, tell me what you think."

"Okay, but I'm still not done reading the latest Nicholas Spark book. It's sitting on my night table in my apartment. I've got to finish it first. Then I promise."

"Good enough."

The women hugged goodbye and Tessa pushed the elevator button to go down to the lobby. She didn't want to admit it to Angel but she was scared, much more afraid than she'd admitted.

"Driver, please wait – I just want to run into this grocery to get some milk," Tessa asked. She didn't mind paying more on the meter, but she wanted to be with someone until she got into her own lobby.

It was two in the afternoon. *Darn it!* Tessa knew she had to rush to get ready for the salon visit. She quickly went into the Third Avenue Deli and picked up a carton of milk as well as some fresh fruit. "Here, keep the change, she said, giving the Korean store owner a five dollar bill." She didn't want to wait on line.

As she exited the store, she felt an ominous presence. Her heart was racing; a chill ran down Tessa's spine. Now she was certain of it. She was being watched. If Ryan Booth was behind this – and he certainly had the money to stalk her, what could she do? This was becoming a ghastly game. Would this ever stop? He obviously had a few screws loose. The man couldn't take rejection, that's for sure. Maybe she should give her sister a call? Tessa didn't know what to do. All she knew was that months had passed and still he wasn't letting go. There was a lot of traffic, the taxi she had asked to wait was double parked was almost in reach, so she ran, opened the door and quickly got in. Somehow she knew she was being followed. Then she saw him – this creepy looking man just staring straight at her as the taxi drove away. She didn't know what to do.

The Next Morning –

Tessa could hear the phone ringing as she showered. She didn't bother about it – probably just another hang-up. Then she heard knocking at her front door. She rang the doorman; there was no answer. Where was the doorman? If no one was watching the front entrance anyone could slip up in the elevator.

She was terrified. If they could get to her front door...what could she do? She knew she was panicking, but how could she remain calm when this had been going on so long?

The knocking got louder. She tip-toed to the front door to try to look out the peephole. There was a man standing there with a delivery.

"Who's there?"

"Special delivery, lady," the man responded.

"Leave packages with the doorman. I don't accept anything here," she responded.

"Come on lady, open the damned door," the rough toned voice said.

"I'm calling 911; you better go away and right now, she said."

Tessa ran back to the phone and called the desk downstairs again.

This time her doorman picked up.

"Dominick, there's some man at my front door saying he has a package," she whispered. "I don't know how he slipped by you, I…."

"Say no more, Miss McMullan – I'm sending Andy up right now. He'll get the guy away. Sorry – we were switching shifts."

A few moments later she heard some conversation outside – the man departed swiftly. And he left no package with the doorman.

Oh, my God! Tessa was scared. Really scared now.

As Tessa finished dressing, the phone rang once again. This time she picked up the receiver. There was silence on the other end. "Whoever this is, you're not going to intimidate me. Leave me alone," she said forcefully, and then hung up the phone. Damn it, she didn't want the creep to know he was getting to her...

As Tessa applied her Chanel lipstick the phone rang once again. This time it was her sister. They were all going up to the family home in Larchmont that weekend and she invited Tessa to join Chrissie and herself.

"I've gotten Mom a subscription to the opera for the season – I know how much she loves it and this way, she and dad will at least have a half dozen nights out together," Katy explained. "He still keeps those damned late lawyer's hours."

"Yeah, I don't know how she stands it. I'm going to get her a bottle of Fendi plus I was thinking of taking her to a play myself. Any suggestions?"

"Sweeney Todd is still playing and doing very well. You know she loves Sondheim."

"Great idea. But I'll ask her what night is good for her before I get the tickets."

"So let Chrissie and I pick you up."

"Are you sure it won't be a bother?"

"Of course not. We'll be taking the Major Deegan Highway, so we have to come up your way anyway. How about 3 p.m. Saturday; is that good for you?"

"It's great, great!" Tessa said smiling warmly. "I love you Katy." She said it and she meant it. She was beginning to appreciate how loyal a sister Katy was. Her old resentments were softening. Life was tough enough.

"Well now aren't we a damn ray of sunshine!" Katy joked. "Hey, I love you too. I'll check in with you tomorrow. And see you on Saturday."

Damn it, why was it so hard for her to confide in Katy? To tell her she was afraid of some lunatic who was stalking her? Tessa knew she had to do something soon, because if it was that Ryan Booth, his sick mind stoked by all that cocaine he was doing was only making him more paranoid, that was for sure.

She would have to do something. She was even afraid of walking out the front door lately. Thank God she had bought that pepper spray. It was better than nothing.

> "Good women are no fun... The only good woman I can recall in history was Betsy Ross. And all she ever made was a flag."
>
> — MAE WEST

CHAPTER THIRTEEN

Wednesday, October 17, 2012

Roger Swanson had spent a goodly amount of time – like a few months now, thinking about Tessa but somehow, after their first awkward meeting, he felt embarrassed – really on edge about contacting her. He'd thought more than once of sending flowers, but no, he didn't want to come off as a twerp. It would have to be a note and then a call...or...damn it, he liked what he had seen, and what happened, and it was his entire fault. Now here it was October and damned if, in spite of everything, he still wasn't thinking about her.

This is absurd! He had easily found her address off Sutton Place. Finally he found the courage to approach her. Well, at least to send her flowers and a card. Unless she was already involved, he was determined to see her again. He ordered two dozen of the most beautiful roses he could find and had them sent to her apartment. He waited all the next day but no response. And the card had cautiously asked her if she'd like to have dinner. Surely just a thank you am busy would be nice if she didn't want to see him?

What Roger didn't know was that after Tessa had received the hideous box of black flowers she was leery of accepting any gift boxes that came her way. Ironically, she told the doorman to leave the box in the lobby. And there it stood all day long. The next morning, as Tessa went down to her mailbox the desk man called her over. "Miss McMullan, on that big florist's box that arrived – there's a card outside, it says "*A gift from Roger Swanson*," so maybe this is from a friend of yours?"

Tessa could hardly contain herself. Flowers from Roger Swanson? She rushed into the package room to retrieve the box herself. Quite a large box at that. It contained 24 beautiful long stemmed pink and red roses, and a small note asking if she'd like to have dinner. Hell no, he had acted like a total turd! She went back upstairs; she had a busy day ahead.

As she was showering, Tessa could hear the phone ringing. Probably just another hang-up. She always waited to learn if there was a message. The light was blinking so there was a recording. She was surprised to hear Roger Swanson's voice. "Hi Tessa, its Roger Swanson. I know I'm a few months late and a lot of hours embarrassed, but I am calling to apologize. I behaved like a real idiot and hope you'll call me back so I can explain. There is an explanation that you might accept, and give me another opportunity to see you. My cell phone number is 212-686-0606. Hope to hear from you."

Damn it. She had once been attracted to the man and now, he was making an apology, however late it took place. Nevertheless, Tessa did not suffer fools gladly and as she'd announced to anyone who would listen – she'd had her fill of these bad-news men. Still, she'd give it some more thought. But he'd have to do more than leave a message apologizing.

As Tessa finished dressing, the phone rang once again. This time she picked up the receiver.

"Hello, it's Roger again," he said politely. "I hope I'm not being a bore. Will you give me a few moments to hear me out?"

"Okay, I'm listening."

"That night we met – well I foolishly took some anti-histamine the day of the party. It was my allergies acting up. Sometimes I can't take the ragweed out on the island in the summer time. I should have known better, Tessa. I was really soused. Taking you to a motel room because I was out of my mind was unacceptable behavior. But I also knew I couldn't drive any further. I am truly sorry. Won't you please forgive me?"

"Well, we'll see. Right now, I'm hurrying out to an appointment. And thank you for the lovely roses," she added softly, letting him know she was interested.

The Week After –

As Tessa turned the keys in the apartment door, she could hear the phone ringing. Tossing her handbag on the reception table in the foyer, she waited to hear if someone might identify their self. Then she heard his velvety smooth voice. It was Roger Swanson.

Within a minute the two were having a pleasant conversation that began with his saying, "If you'll accept my apology, please, for my dumb behavior last summer and allow me to take you to dinner, I promise I won't make an ass of myself again."

"We've all made mistakes," she said with a bit of a lilt in her response. "It's been quite a while but yes, I'd love to have dinner."

"Good, then what about tonight?"

"Well that's fast," she laughed.

"I'll be in your lobby at 7 and we can go to *Atelier* – it's a French restaurant on Central Park South. It has excellent cuisine and a remarkable caviar cart that suits those who are watching their waists, never mind anyone who enjoys a bit of caviar every now and then."

"Super! I've heard about it but haven't been there yet. I'd love to go," she answered, trying not to appear too excited, but oh boy was she.

At seven p.m. precisely, the doorman buzzed that a gentleman was waiting in the lobby. Tessa had thought of inviting him up but knew that the usual reason was to have a glass of something before going out to dinner. No way! That would be a bad idea.

And so, her heart pounding just a little too much, Tessa glided on to the elevator, dressed to the nines in a fabulous new Gucci bronze satin dress. Draped lightly over it, she'd chosen the perfect cashmere shawl to keep the autumn breeze away.

There he was, as handsome as ever, dressed impeccably in what appeared to be an Armani double-breasted suit. Roger looked very distinguished. Tessa was really glad that he'd gotten in touch. Things were indeed looking up.

"We'll grab a cab," he suggested, kissing her sweetly on her cheek, as they strode out of her building.

Tessa was so intrigued and in high spirits she didn't notice a car parked across from her building or the figure inside. It was Ryan Booth, who had been sitting there for the past two hours watching the entrance to her lobby, watching carefully with his steely blue eyes. His disco club didn't begin getting busy until 10 p.m. Why pay a detective when he could sit outside himself and see if he could catch the bitch? Well it worked. He'd lucked out and caught her going out on the town. Who the hell was that she was with? He picked up the Nikon camera with the long range viewer and snapped away. He'd find out. Damn bitch, she'd rejected him for someone else. She will never get away with it. It never entered his psyche that they had only been involved for a month, that it was long over, that she had a right to see whomever she chose. In Ryan's twisted mind she was a woman who had done him wrong, who had hurt him. He was enraged with inexhaustible anger and now seeing her with someone else, a festering jealousy. Gnashing his teeth, he drove off, vowing to make her pay for what she'd done to him.

Tessa was duly impressed Luxurious and modern, Atelier exuded an unmistakable New York energy. The menu by the chef was a balance between French cuisines with some American regional accents. Of course, the ambience was ultra chic.

The well-designed dining room featured a vibrant collection of original art work offset by silk and leather banquettes and tall windows encased in sycamore paneling. Roger sat near her on the banquette, so near she could feel his warmth. She looked at him as he studied the menu and if it wasn't so public, she felt like kissing him right then and there.

"The chef is originally from the Alsace region of France and he creates memorable meals. I was only introduced to this restaurant a few weeks ago. It was at a business lunch. Then I had dinner with some friends. And I thought of you, Tessa, that I wanted to bring you here," he smiled. I'm so glad you came."

He reached over gently and touched her hand with his.

"May I order for both of us?"

"Why yes, I'd like to see what you think I'd enjoy eating," she responded, not bothered at all by his assertiveness. As a matter of fact, she liked his confident air.

"Well then we'll both have the Dover Sole," he told the waiter.

"Very well, sir. And have you chosen anything from our wine list?"

"We'll have a bottle of the 1985 Chateau Laffite," he responded, not paying any attention to the exorbitant price of $265 for the brand.

"We are going to sip lightly," he laughed, looking at Tessa, "and I promise you a glass or two each is all we'll imbibe."

"Splendid. I don't know much about wines but I suspect you've ordered a very good one," she answered.

"We'll let you decide."

"And of course, first, we'll start with some caviar, he said, as a magnificent custom-made Caviar cart was rolled to the table, where the finest selection of Osetra and Beluga caviar, served with blinis and a traditional garnish was set before them.

And so the evening went. Smooth, velvety, soft, romantic.

Tessa was thrilled to pieces at the attention to detail that Roger showed. Yet he wasn't a stuffed-shirt about it. It all came to him with ease.

"Well, I'd say let's make up for lost time, but I'm leaving tomorrow for a business trip out to California. Since we met last summer I've made a few important changes in my life. I'll be gone until November but then there's going to be an art show at the MOMA, and if you can attend with me, I'd be delighted."

"What's the date and I'll put it down right now," she smiled.

"November 3rd, it's a Saturday evening, and actually the first weekend I'll be back in town. "

"Well, then it's a date," Tessa said, just a little giggly from the second glass of wine.

"Let me take you home, now. I have an early morning flight to catch; it's why I wanted to see you tonight. But we'll have more time, I promise you that," he said, as they got up and walked hand in hand out of the restaurant and into the surprisingly warm October air.

Tessa was a little surprised that Roger didn't want to come up to her apartment. But then, she was glad he didn't. They could spend time when he returned, and if things went as well as she felt right now, that was all she could hope for. She was still tingling as she entered her apartment and closed her door, tingling because he had leaned over and gently kissed her on the mouth. Just warm and long enough to make her want more.

Draw a crazy picture Write a nutty poem Sing a
mumble-gumble song Whistle through your comb
Do a loony-goony dance Cross the kitchen floor Put
something silly in the world that isn't been there
before.

— SHEL SILVERSTEIN

CHAPTER FOURTEEN

The Museum of Modern Art,

Saturday evening November 2012

"I used to spend days studying "*Guernica.*" I took a wonderful course at
college, and although it was only one credit, it was all about what just might be
Picasso's greatest work. And I was fortunate. The course was taught by an abstract expressionist artist who really appreciated the work. Oh and, the course
included our reading and discussing Ortega and Gassette's book, *The Revolt
of the Masses*, which illuminated the subject of the painting. There is so much
going on in the painting, so much to learn," Tessa added.

"I'd rather look at you," Roger said, with a twinkle in his eye.

They spent the next hour walking about the exhibit, strolling from room to room at the incredible works of art on display. A special show of great art from some of the world's museums, on loan for the month of November, this was a preview for the privileged few who were members or served on the Board of Directors of MoMA. Tessa was aware that this museum was a place that fueled creativity and ignited minds. It was nice to know that Roger also had an interest in art. Tessa, always fascinated by the visual, had actually taken art history as her minor in college.

She was floating with the dual pleasure of viewing so many breathtaking works of art, and, will wonders never cease, of sharing this experience with Roger. For her, it was almost as if they were in orbit. More than sharing of the art was going on here. *Earth to Tessa, Earth to Tessa, come down here and off that cloud you're on* the little voice in her head whispered to her. *"Oh do I really have to? she thought wistfully."* Tessa loved being in *La La Land*, especially with a partner like Roger.

Two hours had sped by. "Come, we'll get a bite to eat," Roger suggested.

"It's a beautiful night, so let's walk there...it's quite close."

Quite close turned out to be *La Grenouille on East 52nd Street.* Most people knew all about this awe-inspiring restaurant. In fact, it was the first French restaurant to which Tessa's parents had taken her when she was still a teenager.

She was delighted with his choice. It was still one of the most elegant eateries in New York City.

"Welcome, Mr. Swanson, your table is ready," the maître announced in his clipped but velvety smooth French accent.

Tessa realized that Roger had planned this. To take her to this classic French doyenne of sumptuous food...still sparkling after all these years. La Grenouille actually opened its doors on a snowy night in 1962 long before either of them had been born.

After the waiter had taken their order, Roger leaned over in the banquette and gently kissed her on the cheek. Quivers scampered down her spine. Incredible, Tessa was all a tingle from the touch of his lips.

She smiled. To borrow an old phrase, *this is going to be the beginning of a beautiful friendship.* They both could feel it.

God could not be everywhere, and therefore he made mothers."

— OLD JEWISH PROVERB.

CHAPTER FIFTEEN

Walking through the hospital lobby, then the automatic glass doors that led to the exterior of the building, Vera was finally able to get good reception on the cell phone. She was at long last able to talk with Jason, who had been in surgery half the day. She quickly brought him up to date on her mother's condition. "It isn't good; the doctor said my mom will definitely need rehab. She has impairment on her left side, Jason. She can't move her arm, her leg – it's awful," she added, her voice cracking from the strain of the day.

"After a stroke, brain cells die in the affected areas. This results in a variety of physical disabilities, from sensory loss, language disorders, partial loss of motricity, and memory loss. The level of recovery varies from patient to patient. Starting a rehabilitation program as soon as possible is key to recovery."

"Spoken like a true doctor," she laughed. "What the heck is *motricity?*"

"The Motricity Index is used to assess the motor impairment in a patient who's had a stroke.

"My mom has always been such an active person; I know it will crush her to give up any part of her independence." Vera knew only too well that her mother valued her autonomy far more than money, position, anything else in the world.

Vera had just met with the neurologist who provided the details on Anna Stern's condition. "Your mother did have a stroke. There is sufficient loss of movement on the left side that she'll need physical therapy." Fortunately her mother's speech was not impaired.

"Please, don't worry; we'll have her moved down here. There are two excellent rehab places on the East Side. I'll look into them tomorrow. I think Rusk is the best. But we have time. Your mother should remain up there at least a few more days. For safety's sake she has to be observed to make certain there are no more incidents. When I get there you and I can talk with her, to dispel her anxieties. Meanwhile darling, go to the nursing station and arrange private duty nursing. We want her to have every comfort. Try for a nurse that can stay with her from 8 p.m. to 8 a.m."

Vera was relieved that Jason was taking charge. "Thank you; you know how I appreciate all of this. By the way, Tessa has been with me all day. There's no sense tying her up any longer. Should I have her drive our car back to the city and I'll stay with Mom and go back with you?

"Sure, that works just fine. I'll take the parkway and should be up there in another hour. Just winding up here. Have Tessa take the car to our garage, okay? She can catch a cab from there."

"Good idea. No sense her staying up here with me as much as I enjoy her company. She's got an audition tomorrow, that I know," Vera added, her voice fading with the strain of the day.

"Take it easy. I know you're devastated about this," Jason said gently. "Your mother is still a relatively young woman. She's got a good chance, Vera. Strokes aren't such an unusual occurrence. Approximately 795,000 new or recurrent cases of stroke happen annually in the U.S. with about 28% of cases affecting patients under the age of 65."

"Well at least she can speak. I know how important that is to her."

Jason chuckled: "Important to most women."

Vera couldn't help but smile. It was true.

"The statistics aren't that bad. Many patients make full recoveries. We'll take care of your mom and get her the best help available, you know that," he promised.

"Thank you for being here for me and her, Jason. I'll see you later."

"I'll be there as soon as I can. I'm leaving before the main traffic begins."

Vera bit down a little too hard on her bottom lip. The stress was that bad. This was the first time she'd had to deal with illness and for it to involve her mother – a selfless woman who had done so much for her and her brother – this floating anxiety was relentless. She'd have to put on a brave face before she went back into the room. Her mom could always tell what Vera was feeling. She had to let her know that this stroke, it wouldn't be permanent. Oh please, don't let it be permanent.

"Vai is mir!" (1) Her mother spoke softly, resorting to Yiddish, her first language. "Tsures (2) – that's all I'm giving you, my darling daughter. Nothing but tsures."

"Please Momma, don't worry, you're not giving me any trouble. Just rest and get better. I love you so much," Vera said as she leaned over the bed to stroke her mother's forehead. She loathed seeing this tiny sweet figure hooked up to all those wires, to view the scanner above her head, indicating her pulse and heart rate. Vera realized her mother's vital signs had to be monitored; she was in ICU. But no matter what, she couldn't get used to it. To see her mother so vulnerable. This was her stong, hard-working mother who now seemed so frail, so defenseless.

(Footnote: (1) Woe is me. (2) troubles)

"I was able to reach Zach. He's going to come here tomorrow, Mom." Her mother, Anna, smiled. Vera could tell she was pleased. It had been more than a year since she'd seen her son. Zach was constantly busy with his work in D.C. She was proud of his being a congressional assistant; now if only he'd settle down with someone.

"You need to rest. I'll be downstairs in the lounge. Oh and Tessa told me to send you her love. And Mom, Jason will be here in a couple of hours. He wants to see you. He'll find the best course of treatment for you to get better. And I'll be back tomorrow morning, Mom. Please, don't worry about anything," she assured the pallid skinned woman whose hair had long ago turned prematurely gray. Thankfully, her mother had fallen back to sleep.

As she leaned down and kissed her mother gently on the forehead, she hoped she'd hidden her real concerns. *Oh please, God, let her be alright,* was the mantra that kept running through her brain that Vera would be repeating over and over again.

It would take time for Anna to improve. Neither Vera nor anyone—not even the medical staff could predict how long, but in the end it would require more than six months for Anna Stern to regain the full use of her left side. But this was a miracle — some stroke victims never recovered from the complete extent of their impediments, while others had setbacks.

Danken Got! Vera instinctively used one of Anna's favorite expressions... for her dear mother, endlessly appreciative of even the smallest gift in her rather difficult life, was always thanking God. She hoped Anna's resilient nature would help her battle back from this bitter blow – a stroke that might have taken her life.

Meanwhile Jason had already made arrangements to transport Anna at the end of the week to one of the best rehab facilities in New York. The NYU Medical Center's Rusk Institute, a stroke rehabilitation center, offered inpatient treatment. He was determined that his mother-in-law obtain the best treatment that money could buy.

Chelsea, Friday evening in November

"It's nice to see you again," Danny Bianco said, as he got up from the table to greet Angel with a small kiss on her cheek. Danny had picked the trendy Rocking Horse Café on Eighth Avenue, because it was on 20th Street, close to both of their apartments. Besides, he thought Angel would enjoy the inventive, mostly Mexican inspired food.

"Hi. I've heard about this place, but have never been here before tonight. It's nice to try out new places."

"It's really nice, though it does get noisy up front with the active bar trade. But I asked for a table in the back where we can talk, besides eat," he explained.

Angel was apprehensive about her appearance. Instead of wearing the obligatory black shapeless dress to hide any lapses, she decided on the casual, yet high fashion look of the new Ralph Lauren outfit she'd just bought; one that ended up costing her an entire week's salary. It consisted of an appliquéd denim top with delicate eyelet lace edging the heart-shaped appliqués and then a pair of matching denim pants. Still she was nervous. She always felt too fat, too self-conscious of her body.

They ordered from the menu with Danny suggesting that Angel try the chilies rijellenos, a specialty of the house. Good, but with the heavy cheese, she knew she'd gone way past her quota of fat for the day.

Danny leaned into the table and pulled his chair a little closer to Angel's. "Look, I know that the quickest way to make someone defensive is to start a sentence with 'You should...'" he began.

"Well, I should what?" she asked, afraid of his response.

"Angel baby, you've always had a beautiful face and a wonderful personality. But you know I know you for years and well, I've seen you go up and down a few dress sizes but when I saw you the other day, it looked to me like you were settling in on remaining overweight – like you'd just given up."

Angel was embarrassed. Could this man have asked her to dinner only to discuss her overweight issue? She was wrecked out, hurt, shameful that a possible suitor was about to discuss anything at all about her being fat. Suitor? What a fool she'd been to think he had any interest at all in her.

"God allows U Turns," he said. "I don't know if you remember my sister, Carmella, but she was always a little chunky. Well, last year she decided to have the stomach stapling procedure. She was inspired by Carnie Wilson, I think. Anyway, believe it or not, she's lost 100 pounds since then. Angel – she's like a different person – so beautiful – so shapely too."

"So this is why you invited me to dinner? To tell me to get my stomach stapled," Angel said, not waiting for an answer.

Here's ten dollars towards my bill. I've gotta get out of here," she said, tossing a curled up ten dollar bill on the table, then pushing her chair away from the table so quickly, she knocked over her water glass.

"Hey, wait, I'm sorry. I didn't mean it like it sounds. Wait, wait," he said, desperately, as Angel, fled out of the restaurant and hailed the first taxi she could.

Somehow when she got back to her apartment Angel didn't have an appetite. She couldn't bury her embarrassment, the awful rejection she felt even with Haagen Daz or a Sarah Lee Cheesecake, both of which she kept in ample supply in the freezer. She lay down atop her bed, clothing still on, and slowly sobbed herself to sleep.

Angel awakened in a sweat. She lifted her head and peered at the lighted alarm clock. It was 3:10 in the morning. Oh boy, did she feel awful; especially as she realized what had happened earlier. And now she began hurting all over again.

"Please, dear Jesus, help me, help me do something about my weight. I don't want to look like this and I don't know what to do to not down my feelings with food. I've been doing it for years. Oh please, please help me, she cried, kneeling on the floor, and then making the sign of the Cross. *Wouldn't her guardian angel, or St. Jude, or Jesus, or Mary – she was always saying the Hail Mary – wouldn't anyone help her, please?*

It's not about forcing happiness, it's about not letting sadness win.

(UNKNOWN)

CHAPTER SIXTEEN

A few days before Thanksgiving, November 2012

Angel didn't know if she'd have the courage to go through with it, but then again — she was now 55 pounds overweight so what did she have to lose but pounds and then more pounds?

She'd go for the consultation with Dr. Richard Fineman, the bariatric surgeon at NYU who was rapidly building a reputation as one of the best gastro bypass specialists in the city. She'd first read about him in last summer's *Cosmopolitan* Magazine, and after waffling for a while, finally made the phone call to his office. It was an appointment that took two months of waiting before she'd finally see him.

"Frankly, Miss Manelli, I don't know that you're a candidate for *Roux-en-Y gastric bypass surgery.* This is major surgery and carries more risks with it," he said, leaning back in his swivel chair.

"Could you just explain more about it, Doctor?"

There are two important components of gastric bypass surgery: restrictive and malabsorptive.

"With *"restrictive"* – the surgery permanently reduces the size of the stomach to approximately 2 ounces, limiting the amount of food that can be eaten at one time.

Then what we term *"Malabsorptive"* – The new, smaller stomach is attached to the small intestine at a lower point, bypassing most of the stomach and the beginning portion of the small intestine. This means that digestion will not begin until further down your digestive tract, thus fewer are absorbed.

"How much could I lose?" Angel asked hopefully.

The average expected weight loss with gastric bypass operation is between 60% and 70% of excess body weight. This is an average. You may lose more or you may lose less. Maximum weight loss occurs within two years postoperatively.

Most importantly, obesity related diseases such as diabetes, hypertension, gastric reflux and sleep apnea can be resolved or greatly improved within the first year of surgery.

"Then Doctor I'm prepared to take risks," Angel volunteered.

"Let my assistant, Rosemary, give you the facts and the costs of the surgery, young woman. Whether your type of medical insurance will cover it I'm not sure; usually one has to be considered "morbidly obese" for insurance carriers to cover the high cost of the operation."

"Well I'm obese and morbid about it," she answered.

The doctor smiled. He liked her moxie. Still he never dealt with the financial part, but left it to his staff.

Angel was a little shocked to learn that the surgery could cost as much as $12,000 if it wasn't covered by her insurance. And she didn't think the plan they had at her company was that generous. She'd find out but now Angel considered if she might go to her father and ask him for the money. The boat business was a successful one so that might be a way to get it done.

Judi McMahon

Truly, Angel had thought long and hard about it. And also took action. In the past five years she'd been on Weight Watcher's three times, Jenny Craig twice and even tried the nutra-system program for a month of home meals. If there was a new diet book on the market Angel bought it. Her bedroom book shelf was lined with everything from the 17 Day Diet to the latest book by Dr. Oz. While some of them were inspiring, she'd begin with new high hopes, only to go astray. Within three days of attempting to stay on the low carb diets never mind losing ten pounds on the South Beach Diet only to gain back 12 pounds two months later – it was like being a rat, turning round and round on the laboratory wheel – except she didn't lose weight from any of it. You get the idea. The bane of most dieters is that it's difficult to keep the weight off without continuing to count calories and of course, exercise as well. This took a certain amount of discipline. And if the truth were to be known, between her genes and her compulsive overeating, nothing was working.

"Sometimes I'd like to blame it all on heredity," Angel protested. While her three brothers were all tall and slim and most definitely took after their father, Carmine, who at 6 feet and 180 pounds was in good form, she looked more like her mom, who was all of 5'3" and never weighed less than 160 pounds. Come to think of it, when Angel was born she weighed 9 ½ pounds; her baby photos showed her with fat little thighs and double wrists; *'baby fat,'* her mother called it. But that wasn't true at all. Rather, it was like a genetic road map, the fat cells were there and to Angel's way of thinking, there to stay, inviting more to join in. Phooey!

What could she do but pretend it was okay. "Last month I was on the garlic diet," Angel announced to her friends. "I didn't lose weight, but I looked thinner from a distance." The girls laughed.

"Have you ever thought about stand-up comedy?" Vera suggested laughing at Angel's jokes. Which swiftly led to Angel trying out a few one-liners she had memorized: *"How about some of these? You know you're fat when you put mayonnaise on an aspirin. Or you go to the zoo and the elephants throw you peanuts. Or, my favorite this week: Your driver's license says, "Picture continued."*

Not funny. No really it wasn't very funny at all, Angel could readily admit it to herself.

Angel also went through a period of making reminders for herself; banners, small and large of slogans she'd hear about or read somewhere; self-help motivators that she would tape up on her vanity mirror, the bathroom door, and of course, the refrigerator in the kitchen. *Sayings like:*

If you wish to grow thinner, diminish your dinner.

And this one she not only hung up in her room but taped inside her desk at the office:

My advice if you insist on slimming: Eat as much as you like - just don't swallow it.

Oh, if only she could. Angel cried inwardly. She was forever feeling miserable. Yet who did she have to blame but herself? It got so bad that she did attend Overeater's Anonymous Meetings that happened to be held in a Manhattan church not far from her place of employment. But that didn't last long either. Should she resign herself to just being overweight the rest of her life or what?

Nope, it really wasn't a laughing matter. Dressing in black and loose fitting outfits, almost of the time Angel felt self-conscious. She was so uncomfortable with her body image, she rarely looked at herself in the mirror when she was unclothed. Sure, it was the bane of society – yo-yo dieting, articles galore on how Americans were getting fatter and fatter these days. It hurt, it really did. And every time she invested more money and hope in the latest diet program or gimmick, the less she felt able to succeed.

A week later Angel Manelli had her answer. Her insurance plan would NOT cover the surgery. Before she got up the courage to ask her father, she'd look into a cheaper process, the one that was called lap band surgery.

Tedious, all this talk about diets. She knew what a bore it was to anyone. She'd have to handle this on her own. She googled lap band and soon found and on line link to a Westchester bariatric practice that offered a free seminar on the lap band procedure. And best of all, it was on line!

Free seminar

LAP-BAND Explained

The LAP-BAND is a soft, inflatable ring that is placed around the upper portion of the stomach. The band creates a small stomach pouch and slows the passage of food to the digestive system. Simply put, it limits the amount of food that can be consumed at one time and allows you to feel full sooner and with less food. The amount of restriction can be adjusted by increasing or decreasing the amount of saline in the ring through a tube connected to an access port. The access port is surgically implanted beneath the skin and the subcutaneous fat, and is sutured to the fascia – it cannot be seen, and often it cannot even be felt. The LAP-BAND is placed laparoscopically, using very small incisions, which reduces postoperative pain and shortens recovery time.

Benefits and advantages of the LAP-BAND include: Low risk of complications; short recovery time; no intestinal reconfiguration; adjustable and reversible; often covered by insurance.

With a couple of phone calls Angel learned the cost of the surgery was $5,800. This was doable. She had $2,000 in savings; just in case her father wouldn't agree to pay for all of it. Her mind was made up. She picked up her cell phone and called her father at his office.

"Dad, can I see you on a private matter? No, please, I don't want to discuss it on the phone. I could up next Friday afternoon; if you're available we could meet at your office. I have some time coming to me so it would be easy to catch the 1 p.m. train at Grand Central."

Carmine Manelli hung up the receiver. "*Merda! Damned,* but he hoped Angel wasn't in trouble, wasn't pregnant or anything like that! What made him think like that? He knew she was a good daughter, had always been his favorite among his children, and of course, *Daddy's little girl.*

I would rather be ashes than dust! I would rather that my spark should burn out in a brilliant blaze than it should be stifled by dry rot. I would rather be a superb meteor, every atom of me in magnificent glow, than a sleepy and permanent planet. The proper function of man is to live, not to exist. I shall not waste my days in trying to prolong them. I shall use my time."

— JACK LONDON

January 2013

CHAPTER SEVENTEEN

"Momma, you've got schmutz all over your dress," Vera whispered to her mother, gently dusting off the crumbs on her lap.

Maybe she shouldn't have said anything. After all her mother still couldn't hold the spoon well enough with her left hand, and while she was sitting up in the lounge area at the Rusk Institute eating her dinner and seemed to enjoy wearing the new dress Vera had brought for her, half the food toppled off the spoon and onto the new outfit.

Anna seemed pleased to be wearing the dress rather than a robe, and was glad for the blue color. Anna had always loved blue.

"Mom, I spoke with the neurosurgeon and he said you're progressing nicely. Better still, we have the hospital's permission to take you out next Sunday. Jason and I will pick you up at noon and we can go to the park for a while and then we'll take you for a nice lunch."

Anna smiled. "But I'm still in a wheel chair, Vera. Do you think this will be alright and not too much trouble for you and Jason?"

"Don't be silly, Momma. We always enjoy being with you and we're going to take Jason's SUV; there won't be any problem getting the wheelchair into the car. You need to be outside again, to breathe the fresh air. While its January, it's been unusually warm for this time of year and you'll see – you're going to enjoy getting out for a while."

"Oh my darling daughter – my shaineh maidel (4), I'm very proud of you, very grateful."

Her mother's words of appreciation felt very good to Vera. Indeed, she loved the few Yiddish words Anna used. Never mind her Barnard schooling, her now wife-of-a-doctor upper-middle class ranking. She adored the tenderness and intimacy of the terms. Thank God she was given this chance, this seemingly borrowed time to spend with her mother, to let her know how much she loved her. Not everyone gets this opportunity. And Vera wasn't going to waste a moment of it. From now on she'd seize this gift, this pleasure in caring for her marvelous mother.

(4) Shaineh maidel (pretty girl)

The Bod Squad Meets

Angel looked at herself in the gilt-edged mirror and liked what she was seeing. She felt very nearly embraced in the giddy shades of rose and mauve that made up the luxurious ladies' restroom at the Rhiga Royal. It was Sunday, late January of 2013, and while it was little more than three weeks since she had the lap band surgery, she was already feeling so much slimmer. She wondered if anyone had noticed. She reapplied lipstick and then went back to join her friends at the marble topped dining table.

"You're looking very good, Angel," Tessa complimented her.

"I know I was the first one to know you'd decided on the surgery, Vera announced, "But don't feel bad, Katy and Tessa. Angel had talked to Jason and he recommended Dr. Arthur Fineman – who really is an ace in bariatric surgery, so of course, I was privy to Angel's plans ahead of time."

"Hell, it doesn't matter at all, who you told first, or second or third!" Katy said. "All that matters is that you had a safe surgery and that you're now all about getting better."

"And thinner," Tessa chimed in. "And since we haven't seen you in the past month, Angel, I must say I already see a change in your silhouette."

With a big smile, and a tiny tear forming in her eye, Angel was relieved. "Thank you, all of you. I appreciate your support."

"And it's well deserved. You've been a very good friend, Angel, and I'm sure you know that we all love you very much," Vera responded.

"Maybe we should change the name of our group to *the Mutual Admiration Society*," Tessa laughed.

"I'll second that," Angel said. "Though *'The bod squad'* may still fit, and me fit more into the title!"

"By the way, Katy, I never did get a chance to call you but it turns out my mother, who stayed with me the entire week after my surgery, she met your partner, Chrissie."

"Really?"

"Mom went to buy fresh flowers. She's a knock-over for flowers. She is always putting fresh ones in a vase for me, and guess where she ended up?

Chrissie's shop "*The Incessant Gardner,*" is probably the best one in Chelsea, if not in all of Manhattan. And that's where she bought a beautiful bouquet of yellow roses. She came back to my apartment just raving about the floral arrangements, the greenhouse stocked with so many plants and trees and such. I realized it was Chrissie's shop. And when my mom described a tall and beautiful woman, I told her that I think that was your partner."

"Nice."

"I'm going to pay Chrissie a visit next chance I get. I had to get back to work so I really haven't had much time. But I'm eager to see what my mom described as so incredible – boy, did she wax enthusiastic about the place. If she liked it, believe me, she has always had a green thumb – and it was obvious she was impressed, it must be very special."

"Nice to hear, thanks Honey," Katy responded displaying her pride. "Chrissie is very talented and now she is also successful. *New York Magazine* included her shop in their *Best Bets* column two times in the past year and a half. She's always getting good publicity."

"Yes, it's a splendid emporium," Tessa opined. "I went there before the holidays and picked up the most unique and beautiful wreaths, very elegant styles; I singled out four of them – and even choosing four was difficult – they were all that special. I gave three away and kept one for my own front door. It's still up; I can't bear to take it down; it's so spectacular. Chrissie is a very talented woman."

"I'm going to tell her what you've all said. She'll be flattered to hear such nice words," Katy remarked.

"Now how about you, Angel? How are you doing overall?" Tessa asked.

"Oh just great. The witch at my job, our managing editor, is leaving February 1st. "She's going to be the new editor at *L'Officiel* – they're resurrecting the French-American magazine and she went for it. Little do they know what a lack-luster talent she is, but at least she's going to be out of our hair."

"Working for a bad boss is like hell on earth. I've had plenty of division captains and creepy supervisors in my police career that could make our daily assignments repulsive! Especially the loud-mouthed men who think that a badge and a department promotion enlarges their penis as well as their pension. I've had to deal with too many dick-heads in my career," Katy scowled.

"It's well known that men are threatened by strong women. And I imagine that half the men who go into the police department have a need to be little Hitlers," Vera opined.

The women laughed. Then placed their orders.

You have to kiss a lot of frogs before you find your handsome Prince.

— THE BROTHERS GRIMM

CHAPTER EIGHTEEN

A Friday night in February 2013

"Listen, Sadie-lady, I know you were coming on to me at the bar. Why are you playing hard-to-get now?"

"I'm sorry, I made a mistake. I had too much to drink, that's all. I just want to go home. Please. Let me get out and I'll get a cab," Hannah Cohen begged, scared to death. This man who seemed okay when she met him at the *Divine Bar* on 54th Street, the new trendy gathering spot, was now acting like a brute. She wanted to go, to get out of there. Oh my God, what had she gotten herself into?

It was a few blocks from the office and so when one of the copywriters invited Hannah to join her and her friends at this new place, describing it like an advertisement – "*where Tapas was served and the drinks were hu-mongous and happy hour was a good time to meet somebody*" – she thought why not.

Fuhgeddaboudit! That was two long hours ago, and so Hannah ended up sitting alone. She was quaffing down her second pitcher of sangria, feeling a little ditzy, when over walks this refrigerator-size guy, Harley what's-his-name (she never did ask his last name) who had nice dimples, and definitely was the hunky work-out type.

Turns out he worked in construction, lived in New Jersey and the only thing they might have in common was he loved reading Stephen King novels. That's about all Hannah would ever recall of their limited conversation over drinks that night. Yes, he did come on to her, and yes, he was flattering in his compliments, and hell! – It was a Friday night so it didn't really matter if she drank too much.

Now, here she was, in his smelly old Ford Durango. And the doors were locked. "Come on, be nice," he said, trying to put his hand between her legs.

"Leave me alone, please," she uttered. She was inebriated but not half as much as he.

"Come on, you're gonna like it."

Actually she sensed he was also on drugs, he was so damned intense. Hannah tried the door handle. It was locked. How could she get herself out of this horrible situation? She wasn't attracted to this man at all, and now she was in big trouble.

"I don't want to do anything. I want to get out of this car and *now,* " she cried, hoping she didn't anger him any further than he already appeared to be.

He grabbed her tighter, began running his big hands all over her body, squeezing her breasts so hard that it hurt and pushing himself all over her. He smelled too, like he could use a bath. Why did some people not use underarm deodorant and be completely unaware of how they smelled? The unpleasant sweat and odor emanating from his body would knock out a skunk!

Hannah began crying. He slapped her hard on her face. Now she was scared to death. How was she going to get herself out of this escalating nightmare?

"You ball buster!" he said, enraged.

Then suddenly a light came on from somewhere outside the van – it was a flashlight. Then a tap on the window. "Open the door and now," a commanding voice ordered.

It was a police officer and she was saved. He could see that she was crying.

After Harley what's-his-name showed his driver's license to the officer, the cop turned to her and asked "Are you okay? Do you want to press charges?"

"No, please, no. Nothing happened. But I want to go home and he got the wrong signals. I'm so sorry, officer."

"Well, Miss you're lucky I came along. It doesn't look like Mr. Fracetti was taking kindly to your not wanting to be in his company."

That was the first time Hannah had even heard his last name. She hoped it was the last time too.

"I'll get a taxi; I don't live that far away," she said, relieved that this disastrous night was almost over.

"Okay, but I hope you've learned your lesson. Don't get into a car with a man you've just met at a bar. You ought to know better," he warned. He had a teenager at home, a girl. This young woman wasn't much older and he realized she'd had too much to drink. She was in a situation way above her head. It could have been his daughter.

"And you, Yo-Yo head. You're lucky the young lady doesn't want to press charges. I'm letting you go but let this be a warning to you. Keep yourself on the straight and narrow. If a woman doesn't want any part of you, don't force yourself on her or you'll be up on attempted rape charges.

At that very moment, a checker cab happened by and Hannah hailed it. "Thank you officer," she said before opening the door to the taxi. He smiled. "Now get home safely." She gave the turbaned driver her street address and the taxi sped off. She was so relieved to be out of there and totally embarrassed that it had happened in the first place.

⚜

That next day, Saturday morning was a rainy one. Hannah had to talk to someone and Angel, she'd understand.

"I think that every time I put myself in dim-witted situations, I'm creating an ever-widening gap between me and every man on this planet," Hannah said, with resolve.

"Hey, don't think you're the only one. I've had some pretty disappointing experiences myself. Meeting men is easy. Meeting a well-brought-up one is not. One way or another, too many of them are in "la-la" land – piloted by their penises and not much else. Hell, you just happened to meet up with one of the awful ones."

"Awful is putting it mildly. He was a real creep."

"Who was it who said *violence is the last refuge of the incompetent?* " I know I read it somewhere. But that's exactly what happened to you. An incompetent idiot who was frustrated and didn't have the dignity – no – let me say it better – the *balls* to just take no for an answer. So he exploded."

"Oh boy did he go ballistic. Am I lucky that the police were patrolling that area. Eleventh Avenue isn't exactly a great area to begin with."

"Tenth and Eleventh Avenues used to be an area with wholesale butcher businesses all over the place. When gentrification came to the lower Greenwich Village area in the late 1990s, high end restaurants and night clubs sprouted up all over. And soon after that, archaic buildings were tuned into expensive condos, co-ops and high-priced lofts inhabited by the likes of JFK Jr.. The location became known as SoHo."

"But you're safe, Hannah," Angel continued. "You're safe, thank the Lord. And well, I do believe there are some decent men out there. One of them has your initials carved on his forehead – and wait and see – he's going to find you!!"

Hanna laughed. "Oh Angel, you're funny, and so darn naïve. Sorry, but I don't think *Happy Ending* like in the movies happens too often, or that love will find *Andy Hardy* or me."

"Well, give it time. Maybe I'll be proven right after all, Angel said, her eyes sparkling, and speaking in a mere whisper, although it was just the two of them sitting over coffee in the *Tres Good Coffee Shop* on Bleecker Street.

What a lovely surprise to finally discover how unlonely being alone can be.

— ELLEN BURSTYN

CHAPTER NINETEEN

"I thought about inviting Angel to join us for the show – she loves musical comedy and Roger said there'd be no problem getting another seat. But I found out yesterday that she's gone up to Larchmont for the entire week. We spoke briefly – and you're not going to believe this, Vera – her mother has accomplished the mind-boggling feat of the year and gone ahead and asked *Mr. Unfaithful* –better known as Carmine Manelli – for a separation, Tessa revealed. "In fact, she served him with papers to leave the house within a week. That's why Angel went there – to keep the peace."

"Bravo for the lady's courage. It couldn't have been easy. But then, I'm not surprised that Lorraine finally did something about her wandering husband. Everyone knew what a scoundrel he was; he had quite the reputation with the ladies in town. As a matter of fact, years ago, when we were all still in high school, I saw him gallivanting around with one of the nurses from Dr. Stein's office. It was obvious they were passionately disposed. There they were, right squat in the village ice cream shop; he didn't do a very proficient job of hiding his infidelities. It's amazing that it took so many years for Lorraine to find out."

"Sometimes we don't want to know what's going on; it's easier to pretend."

"*Let's pretend* never does work, for any of us."

"Well, Angel's parents aren't the only dysfunctional duo. My mom has stoically put up with my father submerging himself in his law practice. She really doesn't have a soul mate in him; hasn't had his companionship for years."

"I don't know why women still persist in being dependent upon men. *Women's Lib* happened more than 50 years ago, yet men are still in control of the playing field when it comes to love. It isn't an evenly balanced state of affairs out there, no way."

"Vera, I'm surprised you're saying this. After all – you've made a *choice* – to become more independent. We *do* have choices. All of us. Women of our generation have been reared to believe that they can be self-sufficient. Whereas too many of our mothers and aunts and grandmothers are still trapped in the quagmire of traditional expectations; about love and marriage and a woman's role in it. Even now, far too many believe the man should play the dominant role. It's mind-boggling to me."

"It sounds like you've been reading the latest sociology and self-help books. And you're right on point with your facts, Tessa. But reading is one thing, applying what we learn – that's much harder. It can be a slow learn. As a matter of fact, it took me two years too long to figure out that Jason and I weren't right for each other. Much as it would have been easier to sit back and enjoy playing house, I had to take risks. I realized that I wanted to make it on my own, to validate my own reasons for being on this planet, rather than living my life through Dr. Jason Klinghower and his mind-numbing medical career."

"Taking risks is important…there's so much wasted time in too many of our lives," Tessa said. I went through a soul-searching year last year, read self-help books, thought about going in for therapy, and well – I realized a lot of what was holding me back, was me. Then I read a quote from Leo Buscaglia and it resonated with me so much I memorized it. I said it like a mantra for a month or so…and I think it's worth quoting here: *The person who risks nothing, does nothing, has nothing, is nothing, and becomes nothing. He may avoid suffering and sorrow, but simply cannot learn and feel and change and grow and love and live.*

Wonderful, Tessa. May I borrow it and work on this myself?" Vera said happily. "Now let's go get a bite to eat, I'm famished.

" My pleasure, sweetie! And my treat, too."

Selfishness is not living as one wishes to live, it is asking others to live as one wishes to live.

— OSCAR WILDE

....

CHAPTER TWENTY

April of 2013

As she finished applying lipstick, Vera heard the phone ring. It was probably Jason, wondering what she was doing. She picked up the receiver and right away a new argument was stirring.

"You know what, Vera? After all is said and done, no matter how much you want to blame others, I really think you're the one who's out of synch. You carry on like *you have a PBS mind in an MTV world*," Jason alleged, not quite believing it himself, but liking the way his words sounded witty. (He'd read the remark somewhere and thought he'd use it on Vera to make himself sound more adroit than he normally seemed; anything to one-up her.)

"Very amusing. Oh hell, Jason, I've tried for the past year to make things work; to make our marriage better. I've struggled to make allowances for your behavior – why half of the time you are an absolute grouch – and the other half you've returned to your ignoring-me-ways. But it's tiresome. I spend most of the time with my mother, grant you, and maybe I haven't paid enough attention to you these difficult days, but then admit it – you're always working anyway. Work, work, work."

"Work is what allows you to live in the lap of luxury and for us to rent the studio apartment on the ground floor for your mother, Vera. That's what you wanted, in spite of her saying she really preferred to go back to Westchester."

"She's first getting out of rehab and you know she shouldn't be alone yet. This way I can be near her, and I can't even imagine you even questioning this."

"I'm not. I'm just pointing out that my income allows us to pay for her creature comforts as well as our own luxury style of living, so don't knock all the hours I put in."

"Oh Jason, let's not keep arguing. Honestly, I think the marriage counseling worked for a while, but well – we ended up discussing toilet tissue brands and never did resolve our opposing sexual needs."

"Opposing, hhmm? " Jason laughed. "Give me a break. And as far as the toilet paper argument, which was I think a good way to deflect from discussing our real tribulations, well, hell – if your behind is so regal that it has to have 2 ply tissue then buy it yourself. I'm fine with Scott's, which lasts longer too."

"And you had the nerve to tell the therapist that Scotts was better because it didn't hurt septic toilet systems. When did we ever have a septic toilet!" Vera pounced right back. "Come on, Jason. Admit it. You have a cheap streak within you. You'll still look for bargain prices when you don't even have the precious time to adequately comparison shop. That has to come from your mother. I still remember her refolding those slightly soiled paper napkins to use again."

"Leave her alone already. She grew up during the depression. So she's got a built-in alarm signal. Can't really blame her – she had it hard in those days. But then you never really liked my mother anyway."

"Well, she's still too damned nosy and dominating and she has no business telling you that I spend too much money?"

"Where did you get that one from?"

"Okay. I picked up the extension one day. You and she were talking and I heard her myself."

Jason's face cringed. Good thing she couldn't see him. "See that's what I mean. You're spying – just looking for things."

"Well, Dr. Kinghower – even you can't seem to solve our problems. Maybe you could try a different tack? Reduce it to the question: *"How would the Lone Ranger handle this?"* You'd probably come up with as good an answer as either of us has from seeing Dr. Reuben all these months. And at $175 a visit, that's pretty damned costly right there! You know what, Jason? I think the counseling isn't working and neither are we."

"Your sarcasms aren't appreciated, Vera. I've done the best I can and I think you're a bit of a malcontent at that. Spoiled, that's for sure. You should be damned grateful your mother can be taken care of so well and that I want to help."

"Oh I've had it Jason. I don't know how we can get beyond this stress and quarrelling stuff. It's so hurtful to both of us. I'm going over to Rusk to visit my Mom. I'll leave the barbecued chicken for you to eat when you get home with a salad that I made earlier. But later on after Rusk, I'm going to visit with Tessa for a while. I just need some time alone. I hope you understand," Vera said, as she hung up the phone.

The visit at the Rusk Institute went well. Her mother was sitting up, feeling much better. All that physical therapy was working. Soon her mother could come and stay at the studio apartment she'd decorated for her. Now, she'd go spend some time with Tessa. Get a little relief in from all the heaviness.

"Can I trade this marriage in for what's behind door One?" Vera said sarcastically.

"Look, you're under pressure with your mom's stroke and her getting older and more dependent upon you. I wouldn't throw the towel in just yet," Tessa responded. "Remember, just a few months ago you two were doing so well."

"But it's back to the same boring routine, and in bed – well he's really not a thoughtful lover; it's premature ejaculation 95 percent of the time, the man is so into his work schedule."

"Well, I'm neither a doctor nor a sex therapist, but I think those things can be fixed," Tess commented.

"Well then, maybe I don't want to fix it."

"That sounds more like the truth – for once, you're saying something that sounds more candid, Vera."

"I have a confession to make. I've been doing a lot of serious thinking ever since my Mom had the stroke. I thought I wanted a marriage. It turns out I just wanted to be taken care of.

"Welcome to the club. You're not alone, Vera."

"I don't want to trade in the rest of my life to wear Jimmy Choo shoes and designer dresses. I mean, if I can't find a way to earn a good living, with my excellent education, then I don't deserve to have the luxuries," Vera said, getting up and pacing back and forth. "Damned if these heels don't hurt!" she added laughing and sat back down. She took another sip of her drink and continued: *"I want to make it on my own, for myself, moi, me!"* she announced, sounding almost like she was making an "elect-me" type of speech.

"This is so insightful on your part, Vera. And really, with your education and background, you'll have no problem making it, becoming a success at whatever you do."

"Thanks, but with this horrible recession, there are so few opportunities."

"You're right. I have a friend, Leslie, who has a master's degree and lost a good position at ABC TV, after being a producer for five years. She's been out there looking for six months already."

"I'm going to stick it out until my mother is more independent. Then I'm leaving. I'll ask Jason for a divorce and make the terms palatable for him – that I only get alimony for two years – enough time for me to get on my feet and find the right work slot for myself. After that, I want the challenge of doing it all on my own."

"That sounds more than fair to me. But I'm not Jason. And besides, I think he cares about you more than you do him. I noticed how he looked at you at the *Lighthouse for the Blind Charity* Auction last week. He still loves you, Vera."

"I think he loves having me as his trophy wife. I look good. I take him to the right social affairs, which can't hurt his standing in the medical community. But to steal a line from one of my favorite writers, Dorothy Parker, *"You can't teach an old dogma new tricks."* Jason is an old man in many ways, ultra conservative, boring, lives and thinks and breathes cardiology, and I'm just not willing to give another decade to the cause."

"Marriage isn't easy. Even presumably happy couples admit that it takes work," Tessa opined. "Besides the obvious statistics that 50 percent of marriages ends in divorce, I think another chunk of people remaining married aren't happy but afraid to make any moves.

Even my parents. I sometimes wonder why my mother puts up with my father maintaining long office hours. He rarely gets home before 10 in the evening. What kind of life is that for her? I never could understand why she didn't complain, why she seems to settle for so little now that the children are all grown."

"That's her choice, Tessa. She could teach. Your mother is a college graduate, isn't she? They need teachers like mad, even in this economy. That would at least get her out of the house."

"She's trapped in a routine. Bridge and tennis with the country club girls three times a week, and then she volunteers at the nursing home visiting the residents on Wednesdays; she's done that for years and years. She brings them little gifts, helps write letters they want to send to relatives, and makes them more comfortable. But I don't think she'd want to get out and teach. I don't think the thought has ever entered her mind, to join the work force.

"Well, she's still in her 50s; she can still do more if she wants to, while my poor mother – well I just hope she will be able to walk without the walker they're sending her home with. I know she hates it."

"Hey I have tickets to "Death of a Salesman" for tomorrow night.

They're actually a gift from Roger. He wanted to take me but he's not going to be able to get back from Maryland in time. He's working on another building project for the poor there."

"Wow, he's really found a mission in life. It's amazing how much good he's done in so brief a time. And I'm so glad you two are still seeing one another. Do I dare ask......?"

"...No, don't," Tessa said with a slight smile upon her face. "It's good, but I think its better that we take this slow. You're a good friend, so I'll tell you that I do love him, I'm sure of that, but I think I'm going to get that part in the upcoming *Law and Order* show. The audition went well. I still want to try for a career; it's something I want to do, if even just to prove to myself that I can do it."

"I understand. It's like a fire in your belly. Me – I've never really been that enthusiastic about any area of work. Until now. Lately I've been giving serious thought about going into social work. I'd like to work with the elderly. There are more and more people living into their 80s and 90s and soon the older age population will exceed all our expectations. Social security, Medicare, all of these areas are vital and I think I should get involved, either through some kind of legislative role on a local level or through becoming a social worker. I would actually enjoy going back to school. So I'm looking into the options right now."

"So looking for love for you seems to have filtered down to looking for a way to express your love for others. This is very commendable, Vera, and something I never would imagine you doing a few years ago," Tessa said with a sincere respect for what Vera was all about now.

"Thanks. I wouldn't have believed it myself. But we're all entitled to change. And going through this past half year with my mother, seeing all the other older people who are incapacitated because of strokes or suffering from broken hips or need knee replacements that sometimes make them lose their independence, and even their desire to live. *It's a growing problem. I just know there have to be more advocates for the elderly. Our health care system is damned lacking. They're not even giving senior citizens a raise in Social

Security rates for 2013 but the Medicare amount being taken out is going up. Not fair."

"It really is sad. It's a new administration and with all the promises of change, they're still spending on wars and trying to cut benefits to the elderly and the poor. There are so many on fixed incomes, and they stand so little chance of prospering in this great rich country of ours, especially after the Bernie Madoffs ripped so many people off and then Wall Street and the banks also contributed...." Tessa said, trailing off in a hushed silence.

"Not to change the subject matter, Vera, but what about the theater tomorrow night? Can you make it?" Tessa added.

"I'd love to. I think Nichols is a genius and Hoffman a remarkable actor. But I'll only go if you let me treat you to dinner first. I know a very good seafood restaurant in the theater district – La Bernardin. It's on 7th Avenue in the Equitable Building. If you meet me there at six, we'll have enough time to talk, eat, and still make the show."

"Terrific. You're got yourself a date," Tessa said smiling broadly. "I'll be there on time. I think I read a good review not too long ago, by the way. It was in the Times and the writer raved about the fresh food and fish dishes."

"Yup, it's really first class and great atmosphere as well. I'm sure you'll like it."

Little did the two of them know that history would be repeating itself, only with a different cast of characters, when Tessa and Vera set off for the theater the next evening. They'd discover a duo there, one that would be appalling to their eyes and sensibilities and that would change their perspective on marriage and the living of lies.

People change and forget to tell each other.

— LILLIAN HELLMAN

....

CHAPTER TWENTY-ONE

The Chelsea Townhouse of Katy and Chrissie

"I'm sorry we haven't had you over here long before this," Katy apologized. My schedule has been hard and humbling lately, working too many extra shifts; but I'm glad you finally have had a chance to come here, Tessie."

"I'm pleased as well, but not too happy about the fact that it's mainly because of what's happening with Dad."

"Look, it's not the end of the world, and if he's into something life-changing, I'm sure he's hurting like hell right now. I know he's the kind of man who never wanted anyone to know, certainly not his family."

"Then he should have been more discreet. If I hadn't seen him holding hands I would have thought he was having a drink or dinner with an associate," Tessa said, obviously troubled.

"It was meant to happen, hon. We were meant to find out. I don't think there are any accidents in life," Katy said philosophically.

"So you're upset too? It's really a shocker – I mean all of our lives, I never had a clue that he might be bi-sexual – that's what it is, isn't it?"

"I don't know. I'm not a therapist, nor a doctor, and even my own sexual preferences didn't prepare me for finding out my father has more testosterone than necessary," Katy said, taking a sip of her diet coke. "Can I offer you something cold to drink, sis?"

"Not right now, thanks. Just give me your thoughts, please."

"Well, from what I know, the level of testosterone is highest around age 40, and then gradually becomes less in older men."

"Sure – but in the last decade there's Viagra. And we all know older men often use it," Tessa commented.

'I thought he and Mom had a pretty good relationship. They still show affection towards one another. I didn't think his absences were due to anything more than an overzealous lawyer burning the midnight oil," Katy responded. "I'm not a very good detective, I suppose."

"Hey, I don't want to bud in," interjected Chrissie. "But it's probably more difficult to find out something when it's that close to home. Besides, your father has traditionally kept long hours and since his partners are mostly male, it figures no one would give a second thought to any illicit liaisons between him and another man."

"Chrissie is right. There were no obvious clues. You're not a psychic. But if it turns out that this is the case – and Katy, I think it is – you, rather than I, should be a little more sympathetic if Dad's showing a different sexual preference now…I mean…well, you and Chrissie - uhh- you know what I mean," Tessa stumbled on her words.

"What matters most of all now is Mom. What she knows, if anything. This would be devastating to her, if she ever finds out. He's worked hard at keeping this a secret for we don't know how long. So why hurt her now? What good would it do anyway?

You know how she reacted to my *coming out.*"

"Oh yes! That was like a major scene in TV soap!" Tessa recalled.

The brittle mood brought on by the discussion was broken enough for all three women to laugh.

"We've got enough drama going to do a new TV sit com…better than *Modern Family*; more twists and turns," Katy said bemused.

"If this is true, and if it is a pattern with Dad, then we can't let Mom find out anything," Tessa suggested.

"What I think we should do is call Dad and set up a meeting, find a way to talk this out. We do have to keep it hush-hush for now. There's absolutely no reason to hurt anyone. First let's see if he'll tell us the truth…if this is something that just started or if he's been into an alternative lifestyle for longer than anyone realized."

"Well, if he's just new into this, or it's a pattern, he's not going to want to stop."

"You're right, Tessie, he probably won't want to change anything and certainly doesn't want Mother to know. And if this is how it plays out, we can all agree to keep it that way, quiet."

"Then we'll all be living a lie."

"You may be right. Let's see what first happens."

"Look, we're not sure what he'll think about our wanting to meet with him, but I do think if we ask to see him —- perhaps invite him to my apartment and I'll order in Chinese food —- we can talk privately…all of us…avoid embarrassing him…"

"Good idea. I don't know why, but I have a feeling he'll have some idea of what we want to meet about, and, well —- we can start from there. I for one don't want to pass judgment. Both Mom and Dad have raised us to be tolerant beings….so let's just wait and see what he has to say."

"And I don't think I should be there; you all agree, right?" Chrissie chimed in.

"Yup, hon, at this point it's a family affair," Katy said putting her arm around Chrissie's shoulder. "I'm off this coming Monday and Tuesday. If you can call Dad and invite him to your apartment one of those evenings…he should be available."

"No problem. My schedule is a blank; either day will do."

"Hhmmm, wonder if this is telling or not: I noticed the last time I was at the house, in my dad's dressing room area, he had a cologne display worthy of Bloomingdales," Tessa said, obviously bemused. "Come to think of it, he always smells good."

The women had to laugh.

After sitting down over some hot croissants and coffee, Tessa was taken for a tour of the three story home. Between Katy's Third Grade Detective salary, (one in six uniformed members of the NYPD are Detectives. A Detective's 3rd Grade average earning is $100,000) and for Katy, with overtime, this netted her over $80,000 a year, never mind excellent benefits and pension plan. Chrissie's flower business was also doing better than ever with the good publicity she'd obtained. And so the women were able to pool their resources and make a large down payment and bought the Chelsea townhouse on West 18th Street two years ago. From the get-go, they rented the one bedroom street floor apartment with a spacious private garden out to a nice couple. Rents were ample in Manhattan. The $3,000 a month income from this dwelling paid most of the mortgage.

"You do have a really charming home," Tessa said, impressed with the warmth and good taste of the décor.

"That's mostly Chrissie's doing. She's very talented," Katy said, smiling at Chrissie.

"You chose all of the furnishings and did a fantastic job," she added.

"But you're responsible for the superlative art on the walls."

"We were lucky that your father left you all those original sketches, Chrissie."

Chrissie's dad owned an art gallery in Soho. Each year he'd give her a work of art from his first rate collection of abstract expressionists. That Robert Motherwell over there," Katy pointed to the large black and white painting on the dining room wall, "we had it appraised for insurance purposes and it's worth $400,000."

"I prefer the sketches myself....and the Warhol prints are great. Yes, I –, no, I mean that *we* are lucky," Chrissie agreed.

"It's interesting that we both share a love for the abstract expressionists and some of the pop art of the 70s. Dad bought you that wonderful Lichtenstein print and me the coop. I'd never have been able to buy it on my own. And even if I should marry and move out, I can use it as a rental and get income from it. He's been generous to both of us. And the art keeps going up in value. Did you read about the double Elvis by Warhol being sold for 37 million at Sotheby's last month?"

"Kind of bizarre, isn't it? Frankly I can't imagine caring enough to want to look at that graphic image of Elvis, never mind, paying such ransom for it!"

"To each his own," Chrissie added.

"Wasn't it Mom that used to say if we all liked the same man, there'd be a major problem?"

Katy laughed. "It's good that we all have different tastes."

"I'll second that."

"Anyway, we'll get together with Dad and find out what's going on with him. I'm glad you told me what happened, seeing him in the restaurant and I wasn't as shocked as you, but I sort of like Dad the way we thought he was. A *"Father Knows Best"* good guy with his loyalty with Mom."

"But now, we have a surprise for you, don't we Chrissie?" Without wasting another breath, Katy announced: "Tessie, we've decided to adopt a child."

"Wow! No kidding? A boy? A girl? How old? From where?"

Katy laughed loudly. "Slow down, kiddo."

Tessa was excited. "I'm going to be an aunt. And wait till Mom and Dad hear the news."

We want to wait until all the paper work is done. We've been working with the adoption agency for months. We wanted an older child at least of pre-school age. And we're adopting from Guatemala. Chrissie is going there to get the little girl next month. We're going to call her *"Cara Mia."*

"Chrissie, could you get the photos that just arrived from the orphanage?"

In a few moments Chrissie returned with a half dozen candid snapshots of a delightful little girl, dark hair, almond shaped eyes, fat cheeks – a lovely little urchin with a dazzling smile who would soon have a good American home with two women who would love and take great care of her.

"Oh I'm so happy for the both of you," Tessa exclaimed, getting up and going over to each woman to give both a warm squeeze.

"So it sounds like you'll accept our invitation to be her Godmother then?" Katy asked.

"It would be a great honor and privilege; thank you for asking," Tessa said, obviously very moved by the request.

Well now that it's all settled, let me change clothes. I've due in at 9 p.m. for an overnight tour," Katy explained. "And I might as well drive you uptown. We can talk tomorrow about what Dad said and what night you've gotten him to agree to come over."

"Now to get him to agree," Tessa said, not certain at all that her father, who hadn't been up to her apartment in the three years she'd been living in it, would come so readily, especially on his own. She hoped he wouldn't suspect anything. Perhaps they would have to choose a local eaterie; just as long as there was a private dining area.

"A heart is not judged by how much you love; but by how much you are loved by others"

— L. FRANK BAUM, THE WONDERFUL WIZARD OF OZ

CHAPTER TWENTY-TWO

"I've heard only wonderful things about you, Tessa, and I've wanted to meet you for quite some time," Gisele Swanson said softly as she welcomed Tessa into her home.

Without waiting for Tessa to respond to his mother, Roger blurted out: "Yes, Mom, I've found myself a marvelous partner and she doesn't know it yet, but darling," Roger said, turning to an ill-at-ease Tessa, "I want to ask you to be my partner for life, to marry me," he said, taking out a small velvet box from his jacket pocket. "I've loved you for so long," he said as he kneeled down, surprising Tessa and his mother. "I hope, dear heart, that you'll have me."

Trembling, but happy, Tessa smiled. "Oh Roger, I've loved you for a long while too, and yes, I would be honored to be your wife."

"Bravo!" a joyous Gisele said. "And thank you children for giving me this front row seat to your romance," Gisele said, smiling warmly. "Come here; let me give you each a hug."

"Is this really happening?" Tessa said, looking down at the absolutely magnificent and perfectly square cut pink diamond that Roger had placed upon her ring finger.

"Very much so. And now I will have a daughter, which I've always wanted," Gisele added. "I don't know if Roger ever told you that I had two sons; his older brother died in a tragic accident when he was still a child."

"I did tell Tessa, Mom. I think she knows everything about me by now," he shared.

"Well, I might not have told you this, Roger, but I had always wanted a daughter, and about a year after your brother died, your father and I tried; but I miscarried in the fourth month. They told me it was a girl."

"So sorry, Mom. I didn't know and I'm sure this must have been so painful, Roger said, gently rubbing his mother's shoulder.

"Well now we'll have a daughter in our little family, and dear Tessa, I hope you and I can get to know each other very well; that you find me a good mother-in-law, which we've all heard, can be a difficult role to play."

"I don't see that as ever being a problem," Tessa said, walking over and hugging Gisele. She could feel the love, knew that Roger's mother only wanted the best for both of them. How good that was, how lucky she believed their union would be.

"Well, Mom, Tessa doesn't know it yet, but I'd love to have a fall wedding. If you and her and Tessa's mother want to plan all the details, that would be sweet," Roger stated, a big smile on his face. He couldn't have felt happier, more content then at that very moment in time.

"Wonderful! Tessa, let's make a date for lunch. I'd like to take you to my favorite spot, the Café des Artiste. We can talk there and see if you're willing to allow us to make a grand old fashioned kind of wedding – at the place of your choice, of course. And then we can meet with your mom and go on from there."

"Oh of course, Mrs. Swanson…:

"Stop right there, young lady," Gisele interrupted. "You'd make me so happy if you call me Gisele – or even *Mom Swanson* – whatever feels comfortable for you for now.

"Yes, Gisele sounds really good to me for now. And then later, Mom will do. You're such a very special person, beautiful and wise and sophisticated. I hope you don't mind my saying exactly how I feel…this is such a very special moment in my life, and you are very special indeed."

There was a beautiful sense of purpose, of knowing that all of this was right; a mood amongst them that was pure harmony. Gisele was thrilled that her son had found such a beautiful person, inside and out. And the two of them, they were so very much in love. *Wonderful,* Gisele thought to herself. *Finally, my hopes and expectations for Roger are being realized.*

"Now, you two run off to your dinner date. Roger told me he had reservations for Masa. I read the Times review last year. It's supposed to be an unforgettable experience for the best in Japanese sushi. A good choice, for this very special day!" Gisele enjoined.

"Thank you for all your compliments. I hope I can live up to them. Roger, can I call my parents right now? Before we get to the restaurant? And I'm dying to tell my sister Katy. Let me borrow your cell phone please, I forgot to charge mine and it's almost dead!" Tessa said joyfully.

Later at the restaurant and over a ginger and mint green tea, Roger spoke: "It's amazing, sweetheart, how my Mother came out of her shell; her bottomless melancholy. Every since I told her about you, she's been acting cheerful, hopeful in a way I haven't seen her in years. It's like you're a wonderful ray of sunshine that has brightened both our lives. Thank you darling."

The rest of their evening was sparklingly blessed with all things loving.

The next day

Tessa had loved her time alone with Roger, the restaurant, the ambiance, the knowledge that they would spend their lives together. What a glorious happening, so much, so very, very much for which to be thankful. But now she'd have to meet with Katy and their father. She hoped this wouldn't be too painful for any of them. As to Tess – yes, her father would be walking her down the aisle. Her father who had admitted to Katy and Tessa, that, all right, he had a young lover; that this wasn't his first extra marital affair, but he really did spend most of his time working on cases at the office.

This was disclosed the next evening when Tessa and Katy met their father at a nearby restaurant. It was a location where there were quiet areas in the back, and where they could talk in privacy.

Their father came right out with it. He and Jim Larsen, a new intern at the firm, they'd became involved about two months ago and now spent one night a week together. He assured his daughters that while it was cheating, he had respect and love for their mother. "I know this is morally wrong. I know I'm being unfaithful, but I've fought with my own conscience about this for years. I even saw a shrink for 10 months. We were married 26 years before I gave in to my *'other side'*. And, I always practice safe sex. That is uppermost on my mind."

"You were seeing a therapist? That's probably more shocking than our finding out about this romance you have going *on the side,"* Katy said.

I have no defense. I want to continue the outside dalliances – that's all they are, believe me. I truly love your mother; have loved her from the day we met. She's one terrific lady and there's no way I want to hurt her."

"I accept this, Dad. I don't understand, but I don't think that has a bearing on your choices. It is *your* life to lead," Tessa sighed.

"I hope you can balance your personal commitments, your time with Mom, and this other issue," Katy added circumspectly.

In truth, both women were disappointed. Even Katy, who might be more accepting really wished her parents would have remained an old-fashioned and traditional married couple. Life certainly was filled with surprises.

"Good enough. Now let's order something to eat before the waiter, who has been to our table three times in the past half hour doesn't think we're deadbeats."

While Tessa really didn't have much of an appetite, she ordered the fish dish of the day. She was determined to make this into a constructive learning experience.

"I'll take the red snapper," she told her father, who was ordering for all three of them. He was forever the gentleman; she'd always admired his good manners.

"Very good, darling. And I'll order some guacamole; we can all dig in until the entrees arrive." Both girls remembered back to their weekly visits to the local Mexican restaurant in Scarsdale. It was a family affair and everyone loved the guacamole. So much had changed since then. But they had to stay in the "Now."

Tessa shared with her father all about Roger and their getting engaged, feeling good that there was something pure and positive to share. Yes, her father would be walking her down the aisle. Her father who had admitted to Katy and Tessa, that, all right, he had a young lover; that this wasn't his first extra marital affair, but he really did spend most of his time working on cases at the office. This was the time to be accepting, a lesson not always easy to apply.

"Life is what happens to us while we're busy making plans" wasn't that the proverb her mother always said when there were disconcerting circumstances arising in any of their lives?

"And now, Dad, I also have a surprise for you," Katy said, opening her handbag and taking out some new snapshots of Cara, the little girl she and Chrissie were adopting. "It's good news, too," she said smiling. She handed the photographs over as she began to tell her father about the little girl who'd be coming to live with them in just a few more weeks.

A part of you has grown in me.
And so you see, it's you and me
Together forever and never apart,
Maybe in distance, but never in heart.

....

CHAPTER TWENTY-THREE

"The shower is at my apartment. Next Wednesday at 7. I hope you can make it, "Angel said, inviting Hannah Cohen to join a group of women friends who were coming to celebrate Tessa's upcoming marriage.

"Of course, I'd love to be there. And I'm so sorry that I didn't RSVP to your invite. I've barely had time to breathe since I finished the book and found an agent who loved it so much, she's gotten me a contract with Simon and Schuster – and a fabulous cash advance of $25,000 – which I'm told is pretty good for a first novel."

"Whoopee! I can say I knew you when!! Oh Hanna, I'm so happy for you.

This is really super duper," Angel said. "Congratulations. It couldn't happen to a nicer person."

"Yeah, but you can't go to bed with a book. I'm still looking for someone to share my life with, someone to love. It's isn't easy, looking and looking and looking for love – too often for me in all the wrong places."

"Where have I heard that before?" Angel said, laughing loudly.

"Well it isn't easy, it really isn't," Hannah added with a sigh.

"Keep on looking, babes, never ever give up. I met Tony through you, you know that. And we're still seeing one another. I don't know if I'd say it's all rockets and stars, but he's my first boyfriend with whom I feel protected and loved. He's really a nice guy, Hannah, and I'm thankful you thought of me – to bring me along to his party.

"Yes, Tony is a great guy. And you know, he's thriving on Wall Street, even during these hard economic times. But you don't sound that passionate about him and I think crazy passion – a real craving from deep down into the pit of your stomach, no, the pit of your soul –that what you should feel when you first fall in love," Hannah commented.

"Spoken like a true romantic."

Hanna giggled.

"You might be right," Angel commented. "He's nice, thoughtful, and yet – well no bells go off, if you know what I mean. But I'm not throwing him back; he's the first man who is worthwhile after I lost all the weight. I'm sure he'd never have looked at me last year. And well, now that I'm feeling good about myself and we're having fun, I just want to enjoy the journey for a while. There doesn't have to be a destination for everything in life, now does there? And yes, you're probably right, Hannah. I don't think he's the one I will end up marrying."

"Have you considered that maybe; just maybe you might have cold feet about marrying anyone after everything that's gone on with your parents? Every time you call and tell me about their problems and about the separation," Hannah paused, "anyone could tell how painful it's also been on you."

"Well, now, you're going to get a kick out of this new turn of events," Angel said with a big smile on her face. "My father moved in with his mistress two months ago and now he's been begging my mother to take him back! He said he misses her; that he misses the family life, that, believe it or not, he's finally willing to give up the entire affair."

"Unbelievable! Sounds like once he moved in and could see the real difference between his mistress and his wife, he values your Mom. Truth can be stranger than fiction. If I wrote this into my novel, who would believe it? What a wild soap opera!" Hannah giggled. "So come on, tell me – will your Mom take him back?"

"I'm not sure. She ended up enrolling in courses at the community college and now she's thinking of going to college full time."

"Terrific!" Hannah exclaimed.

"She's changing, after all those years of being an old-fashioned wife, she's actually changing and getting to be a lot more independent. As a matter of fact, the last time we spoke, she actually said, *"Let him dangle in the wind a while, then I'll decide."* I couldn't believe my dear sainted Mother would sound so assertive, so sure of herself! I tell you I had to hang up as fast as I could so she wouldn't hear me laughing; I wanted to give her assurance and no thoughts that she couldn't really do whatever she wanted. It's amazing, really amazing!"

"Hope you'll let me know what happens," Hannah added.

"Of course I will. And whatever it is, I have a feeling it will be for the best for both of them."

"Well, now, why don't you tell me what Tessa might like as a shower gift – and I'll get it?" Hannah changed the subject. "I'm sure she's loaded down with Victoria's Secret stuff. I was thinking of maybe just getting her a deliciously soft terry robe or something more practical like that. After all, she's the girl who has everything!"

"Well, I've gotten her two gifts. One is a really conservative choice. It's a book by Dr. Laura called *"The Proper Care and Feeding of Husbands.* It's a hoot!

Should make for a few laughs. And I also bought her a beautiful buttery soft Coach wallet that I know she'll like. It's her style lately – which is definitely more traditional since she's become engaged. Tessa is wearing less sex-driven clothing – no more outrageous high heels with spangles on them, and definitely higher necklines. Funny, isn't it?"

"Sounds like she's really into him. You know I remember reading a quote a long time ago from Gloria Steinem that I think describes what Tessa is going through. It was: *The first problem for all of us – men and women – is not to learn, but to <u>unlearn</u>.* I think Tessa is growing through these subtle changes and unlearning some of her less attractive habits. And of course, I also envy her getting hold of such a terrific catch. Roger Swanson is definitely a winner – a gorgeous guy with money and with his latest projects of building housing for the poor – he exhibits a real desire to do good deeds. She's very, very lucky."

"I'll second that. And I think she deserves him. She has a good soul and I've never seen her not stop and help someone in need. Tessa keeps dollar bills handy and I swear whenever she sees someone homeless, she offers the money before they even ask. She does care about others," Hannah said with admiration.

"Yes, I remember her helping out at my Mom's church auction last year. She came early and stayed late to help clean up. Wow, we've been talking for 10 minutes already – I've gotta go now. But I'll see you on Wednesday," Angel said, saying a quick goodbye as she hung up the phone. She had to get back to writing copy for a new fashion spread for the magazine: the new Ralph Lauren collection. Life was good, she felt great and even her roaming two-timing father – he really seemed ready to change his ways.

"Oh dear God, why, why did this have to happen? My mom was doing so well, she was beginning to walk around on her own," Vera said, crying as she was telling Tessa the shocking news. She'd just finished a phone call from the health aide who visited with her mother each afternoon. The aid had found her mother sitting up in a chair, quiet, too quiet. She was dead. Her dear, wonderful mother had died. "I am sick over this, but at least she didn't suffer. Jason left his office to go over to the apartment. He'll take care of things. We think she had another stroke, but I told him, no autopsy, leave my mother alone. She's gone, but now she's with my father, who died far too young, and now she's gone too." Vera could hardly speak, her voice was shaky and she was sobbing.

Tessa was having problems understanding Vera's words; she was crying so intensely. "I'm coming right over. I'll help you in any way you need help. Just wait and take some deep breaths. Make yourself a cup of tea if you can. Wait for me, please and I'll go with you to the apartment."

"Thank you. I could use a friend here," Vera sobbed. "Jason said he'll sign the death certificate so they won't take my mother to the morgue or anything like that. I've got to make funeral arrangements. In our faith, the deceased have to be buried quickly. There's a plot at Zion Cemetery in New Jersey. That's where my dad is interred. I'll have to call there and also a funeral parlor and…."

"Take a deep breath. Don't do anything. It won't take me more than seven minutes to get over to you, midtown traffic or not," Tessa interrupted her friend, who was crying hysterically.

"Alright, I'll wait," and with that Vera gratefully hung up the phone. She ran to the bedroom to lie down to cry her heart out. It hurt so much, to lose her beloved mother. She couldn't even call Zach – anyone else. She'd wait for Tessa to get there.

Two days later on Thursday of that week, with a nasty downpour, and with a cold and bitter rain coming down, there was a funeral with a Rabbi, who really never knew Anna Stern, giving a fleeting history of the life of Anna Stern, as told to him by her children. He spoke of this plain, honest, loving woman who always was a good woman, and then both Zach and Vera spoke briefly. Then a caravan of cars followed the hearse to Mt. Zion Cemetery in New Jersey. It was bleak and dark and black and cold that day. Poor Anna was only 64 years of age. She'd had a hard life and now when her daughter had only started to make up for some of the lost years when she didn't pay enough attention to her gentle and good-natured mother, her mother was gone.

"Oh Zach, I hope Mom knew how much she was loved. It's hard not being able to say *I love you* any longer," Vera whispered to her brother, whose eyes were red with the traces of crying, knowing he too had not spent enough time with his mother these past few years he was busy building a career. He would say *Kaddish* at the cemetery, but Zach had to be at work that week; he would not do the traditional sitting *"Shiva"* which close family members did for five days in respect for the dead. Vera thought Jason wouldn't sit either. How awful. But there was nothing she could do. Nothing. Still she would sit, cover the mirrors, and friends did stop by.

Surprisingly Jason did take the first two days off and sat with her as well. Sitting Shiva gives everyone time to reflect. And for Jason this turned out to be more about him and Vera's marriage than anything else. A morass of maddening thoughts was flying through his head. He was all caught up in regrets and confused emotions. He had to be there for Vera, for her mother, but their marriage was a shell, an empty nothing. Jason knew she wanted to complete her masters and that they could go on living like they were, almost like roommates, but it wasn't working for him, no way.

After the mourning period was over, he'd have a heart-to-heart talk with Vera, and discuss his moving out. But right now, he took a couple of days off, rearranged his surgeries. He owed her that and she did deserve tender and loving care. Oh, if only it could have been different, if their marriage could have worked. Quietly, he allowed a few tears to trickle down his cheeks; Vera, if she noticed at all, would think he was mourning her mother's passing. At least he hoped she'd never know how bewildered he was that their marriage was over.

Friends came and brought fruit and platters of sandwiches and such. Those who remembered Anna Stern were especially saddened that she died so young.

Vera lighted a *yahrtzeit* candle which is done in memory of a loved one and kept the candle going with another and another all through the period of mourning to honor the memory and soul of her mother. She talked and talked to anyone who would listen about the wonderful traits of her dear departed mother, until she was hoarse and tired and knew there was nothing left to say.

"Life is what happens to us while we're busy making plans." That phrase played over and over in Jason's mind. He was sitting next to Vera on their oversized velvet couch. He leaned over and gently rubbed the back of her neck. "I'm sorry kiddo, I'm really sorry," was all he could say.

"If you want a happy ending that depends, of course, on where you stop your story"

— ORSON WELLES

CHAPTER TWENTY-FOUR

"Welcome to Tiffany & Company's Wedding and Gift Registry," the slickly dressed and well-rehearsed counter salesman proclaimed. "We're delighted to be of service." Ta Da! The only thing missing were the sounds of trumpets blaring.

"If you love beautiful things, registering with us is easy and will be a rewarding experience," the tall, lean and positively handsome young man added. (He was a looker – it went with the Tiffany milieu.)

These welcoming words were faultlessly spoken by Derek Johnston, a wanna-be actor who had made it all the way from Okefenokee, Illinois to New York City to establish fame and fortune on the great *White Way*. To date, and after two long years of walking the pavements and auditioning daily for roles, all he'd garnered was one gypsy part in an off-Broadway musical. That wasn't nearly enough to make it in the *Big Apple*, never mind being able to support himself. And so when Derek ran into a particularly dry period and couldn't find any work – he took the advice of a fellow dancer and joined Tiffany's. He had the right looks and demeanor (and he certainly had enough bills to pay).

Derek was of the opinion that it was a thankless job, but when he had to excuse his present position to his friends, (after all, working as a lowly salesman wasn't exactly what he'd expected his life would turn into) he'd kid about it, and, if hard-pressed to explain his present status he'd explain that he had "*a lot of Karma to burn off.*"

"I'm in between jobs but up for a part," was the accepted mantra of the out-of-work actor who needed to wait tables or drive a cab or better still acquire a superior-to-thou job at a high end establishment like Tiffany's. And because Derek needed to pay $75 an hour for his new voice coach, never mind to whittle down his credit card bills, for now, he'd gladly remain at Tiffany's until a good role, no, come to think of it, any role would do.

Tiffany's elegant Fifth Avenue superstore was the backdrop this warm August day because the soon-to-marry duo of Tessa McMullan and Roger Swanson had decided to establish a registry for themselves. Greeted by Derek Johnston, and appropriately enrolled, they were now wandering hand-in-hand through the fine china and sterling silver section of the posh Fifth Avenue store making their selections.

"Would you like me to share a little secret, Roger?" Without a moment's hesitation Tessa continued: "I'll always cherish the initial misconceptions I had about you," she whispered playfully in his ear. He grinned. She was lightheartedly teasing him as they walked around, taking notes on patterns before entering their choices of sterling flatware and china place settings. Remarkably, they had the same taste for simple lines.

"I detest "*Bronx baroque or early nouveau-riche renaissance,*" Tessa joked. She was in an exceptional mood of jollity and wit, for now all was right with her world. Her long flight of fortune on looking for love was finally and fruitfully finished. She'd found it in Roger and there wasn't a day that went by that she didn't thank God for him.

Besides all of this, Roger had stunned Tessa by purchasing a wonderful three bedroom high-rise. After their marriage in October, they'd be moving into a beautiful 6,000 square foot residence at 730 Park Avenue, an ultra luxe building. Furthermore, the rigid board of directors didn't approve just anyone. The Swanson family name and connections, never mind the money that Roger brought to the table, would assure the couple of immediate approval. "We can live there happily – at least through the first baby," – he announced, kissing her affectionately on the forehead. He meant it; he wanted to have a family. Tessa liked the idea of beginning a life of some domesticity; yet she wanted more.

"You know they're calling me back for a read-through for the *Law and Order* role. I hope you understand that I still want to pursue acting," she said with a serious insinuation that was also saying *"don't challenge me, please."*

"I couldn't imagine having it any other way, darling. Act to your heart's content, and if you get bigger and better roles, let's deal with that as it happens, alright? I'll support your dreams as you're supporting mine. Always know, dear Tessa, that we're a team."

"To hell with propriety," she decided, stopping right then and there in the sterling silver tea service section and planting a long passionate kiss on his lips. Out of the corner of her eye, Tessa noticed two Tiffany shoppers smiling. Expressions of love **were** appropriate anywhere. And Tessa was blissfully in love.

Early September 2013

"Thank you Carmine, the flowers are beautiful. But I dunno, I dunno if I can handle any of this anymore," Lorraine was saying. She'd agreed to meet her estranged husband for dinner at one of their favorite restaurants, *"Luigi's"*—they'd dined there years before when they were dating and every once in a while, they'd go back. Carmine had brought a large bouquet of scarlet red roses, flowers he knew she would like. He certainly knew how to be the charmer when he wanted to, but it was no longer enough.

Long-suffering, tired of appearing like a dithery, squawking, hysterical housewife and after looking in the mirror and going for some much-needed counseling, Lorraine Manelli was determined to show a new strength and security. After all she'd been through this past year and then some – she'd become plucky, clever and most resolute in her new-found feminism. And she'd be damned if she'd give an inch to her self-aggrandizing husband.

Scrutinizing the initialed shirt sleeve cuffs, the Versace sun glasses, the silk handkerchief in Carmine's pocket, Lorraine couldn't help but thinking – *"damn it – he's still preening himself like a peacock with a puffed-up ego."*

She would use whatever leverage she had at hand to hold her own. And, no, she wouldn't be subjugated to the old time advance-and-retreat game – the way she and he used to deal with one another. Because then he *always* won. Finally, Lorraine Mannelli had become a disciple of the new feminism she'd disregarded for years. She was sick and tired of their worn-thin traditional union. She was finally willing to spar with her husband for what she wanted. And what she wanted was a real partnership or to hell with it all.

"Damned, if being sexy was a crime, you'd be guilty as charged," Carmine opened his argument as he reached for Lorraine's hand.

She quickly withdrew her hand: "Look right now, any connection between your reality and mine is purely coincidental. I haven't sat on my ass these past eight months, Carmine. I've been busy growing up. Now if you have something to say, say it, but please, let's not have that kind of false flattery."

He couldn't believe what he was hearing. She even embroidered her sentence with an *"ass."* Carmine turned beet red. "Look, I was wrong; I admit it all the way. I'm getting a little long in the tooth. I give up!!!! I don't care to stray any longer. I promise you I will give up any outside affairs. Roseanne and I are over. I gave her a pay-off package. She's not even working in the business any longer. I swear, Lorraine, it's true."

"So what does this mean for you and me?"

"I want to come home. Roseanne, she was nice about it all. She came in to the office for two weeks and trained Joe Brazanni. You remember him? He's Nick Brazanni's son and he needed a good job. I'm starting him out at $5,000 more a year than he can get anywhere. I love ya, Lorraine, I love ya," Carmine said, tears forming in his eyes.

Lorraine couldn't believe what she was hearing. He was like really repentant. After all those years he'd given up Roseanne; did she hear right? – did he really break up with her? Lorraine knew how important Roseanne was to Carmine's business; she'd worked for him so long she knew how to run everything. Was it for real – that he was giving her up and was doing it on his own?

"I swear on our children's lives, it's over! I did it, almost a month ago."

"Oh Carmine, if this is true, if you can remain a faithful husband, then yes, yes, I want you to come home," she said, melting at the prospect of getting her husband back for good.

"It's gonna work out Lorraine. I already went to see Father O'Malley *twice*. He's listened to my confessions and he's also guiding me. I want to be with you, to spend the rest of my days with you. I love you, truly I do."

With a humongous sigh of relief Lorraine responded: "That's good enough for me. Come home, come home," Lorraine said, as she took her hand in his and held on tight.

"Well now, doesn't this seem to be a miracle?" Angel exclaimed at hearing the good news from her mother. "Looks like it's going to be a happy ending after all. I've been praying, praying every day, but to tell the truth – I didn't have that much faith and yet it's really happened. Oh, momma, this is wonderful, simply wonderful!"

"Will you come to dinner next Sunday?"

"I would but that's the day Tessa is going to be married. I'm one of the bridesmaids, Momma. And my dress is a size 8! Can you believe it? I now fit into a size 8 and my weight, it's at 120 pounds. Oh Momma, everything has changed for the better. I so want to see you and daddy but not next weekend.

How about the following Sunday? I'll be able to see all of you that Sunday, if it's okay with you?"

"Of course, sweetheart. "I'll make a seafood dinner. I know how much you love lobster and shrimp and clams and I'll prepare the usual macaroni dishes too, and I'll," Lorraine interrupted herself. "I still love being the cook of the house, women's lib or not!" she laughed. "But you know something, Angel? I told you first but wait until your brothers hear the good news! I've gotta hang up and call each of them. Oh this is so exciting. I'm so very happy that your father is changing his ways and will come home for good."

Angel sighed with relief. She was thrilled at the news. "Momma, I'm going to call Daddy and tell him how much I admire his decision. I think he's really done a 100 degree turnaround. You know he always seemed to have a roving eye."

"I know it darling; I just pretended it wasn't true. But I suspected all along…it was just better to believe in my fairy tale. But now, now things are really good, thanks be to God and Mary and Jesus and all the Saints above," she said with deep conviction.

"Wait, don't hang up yet Angel – give me Tessa's address. I want to send a gift from Daddy and me. Or if she has a gift list somewhere…."

"Of course she does. At Tiffany's; the main store on Fifth Avenue. You can ask for the Tessa and Roger Swanson gift registry there and decide what you want to send."

"With pleasure. And of course, some day, if my prayers are answered, my darling daughter, your wedding will be the next happy event."

"From your mouth to God's ears!" Angel said laughing.

Angel put the receiver back on its base. She was thrilled for her mother. No sense bursting her bubble by telling her that she'd decided to end her association with Tony. Tony was a good guy, but she had finally accepted it –he was not for her. Worse, lately he was getting far too serious. She felt suffocated. No sense staying in something that wasn't right. She'd seen the anguish her mother had gone through with her father's unfaithfulness. She'd witnessed the heartbreak of Vera deciding to leave Jason. And she'd experienced enough disappointments in the relationship area to know that finding love, true love, wasn't that easy. She told Tony gently, but firmly, that it was over, for both their good.

Angel would once again be on her own, once again looking for love. To paraphrase a quote from one of her favorite writers, Dorothy Parker, Angel knew eventually she'd find the right one, but until then, she had no intention of *"putting all of her eggs into one bastard."*

I've never been a millionaire but I just know I'd be darling at it.

— DOROTHY PARKER

....

CHAPTER TWENTY-FIVE

Sunday, 9 a.m. at the Pierre Hotel

It was fantastic having *the* hairdresser to the stars, Lance Christopher, owner of the luxe Beverly Hills salon carrying his name; fly in with his staff to perform all the makeup and hairstyling for Tessa and the members of her bridal party. Lance was an old friend of Gisele Swanson, who had arranged for this very special visit and of course, paid for the private plane and services of the staff. She was overjoyed that Roger was marrying such a lovely young lady.

"And then the traveling salesman ran out the door and straight down the hillside before the farmer could get to him with his pitchfork," Angel ended her tale, telling one of the more raunchier jokes of the morning. Everyone laughed. It was a silly time, a time to let go and relax.

Most everyone was giggling with anticipation inside the spacious three-room suite that had been set aside to take care of hair, makeup and last-minute nail touch-ups. Even Vera, known for her acerbic wit, seemed mellowed by the marriage that would soon take place. After all, everyone loved happy endings. And while she and Jason had parted, they'd parted friends. He was a decent man and a very dedicated doctor; she'd always admire and respect him. Concerning her goals – becoming a more constructive person by opting for a career working with the elderly – was already becoming the most fulfilling part of her life. After too many years of ennui, the superficial designer fashions, the empty days and nights, finally she felt worthwhile in finding something that really mattered to her – helping others.

As for Tessa, she couldn't have been happier. Friday night had been the pre-wedding dinner party. Everyone who was dear to her and to Roger, both their friends and family – all were present and readily celebrating this happy union. It was at the dinner that Gisele Swanson stood up to toast the couple and gave Tessa a diamond heart necklace to wear. "They say something old and something new – this is *very* old. Roger's father gave it to me when we were dating. I can't think of anything more precious than this to give to you, Tessa, to wear on your wedding day. And for you to pass on to your daughter."

"Oh thank you so much," Tessa said, as she walked over to embrace her soon-to-be mother-in-law.

"Call me mother won't you?" Gisele asked.

"I would be honored to do so. Yes, thank you mother for this beautiful something-old to wear. You are a precious person, and I'm so grateful that in finding Roger, I have also found you."

Everyone applauded. Vera took her desert spoon and gently rattled it against the crystal water glass. "Here, here. You are both very lucky."

"And you, dear Roger, you can call me mom or mother – whichever you prefer," Tessa's mother said. "Now let's toast the happy couple," she added lifting her wine goblet into the air.

Everything seemed so good, so perfect. Little did Tessa know that at a dining table across the room one of the patrons had been cagily watching the wedding party as well as snapping pictures with a miniature camera. A wanna-be investigator, Scott Malone had been hired by Ryan Booth and given orders to learn and record all he could and to report back with the details by midnight. For $500 it was more than worth it. What did he care what the man wanted the information for? Just getting an assignment from a well-known disco club owner was good enough for him. It would look good on his resume. Little did he know.

Ryan Booth had learned about the hotel and the wedding plans since first reading the announcement in the New York Times. He had bided his time. It was getting near to when he would strike. He had to let this bitch know she would have to pay for what she had done to him. No, she wasn't going to get away with it. And getting her on her wedding day would be just what the doctor ordered. His nose had long ago healed, he looked as good as ever, but she had more than wounded his pride. She'd repeatedly refused his apologies. That would never do for a man of his self-conceit and arrogance. Women were not to be trusted and this one was a real bitch. Now she was trying to marry someone who was filthy rich. Crap! Not so fast. He'd make her pay for his long months of suffering.

It was 10 a.m. before Tessa's makeup was finished. As she started towards the next room in the suite where Lance was waiting to place her golden strands of hair up and into the unique hairdo he had created especially for her for this very special day, she remembered she wanted to make a phone call.

There was just so much tumult inside it was hard to talk. Deciding to use her cell phone she stepped out into the hallway. Tessa walked a few feet down from the suite to have some privacy. She wanted to call Angel's mom and thank her for the beautiful silver tea set she had sent over from Tiffany's. It was truly dazzling.

As she began pressing the buttons on her handset she noticed a man way down the hall walking through the sumptuously carpeted hallway pushing a service cart. She thought nothing of it until he was a little closer and then she began to think he looked familiar – like the man she had seen a few times following her in the street.

No sooner did this instant recognition hit her than she noticed the man was reaching under the cart to pick up some kind of a can. Tessa sensed something was wrong, terribly wrong.

There was no one else out in the long hallway of the hotel. Then suddenly: "You bitch!" a voice said as she was catapulted around – the man had slowly but surely come right on up to her and it looked like he was about to throw whatever was in that can at her. *Oh my God, what's happening to me?* She thought, quivering with fear.

Without Tessa realizing it the emergency door to the hall stairs had bolted open. "Move away from her. Now," someone shouted. Another voice commanded: "Let go of her."

Tessa was frozen with fear. Time had suddenly stopped. It was like a movie where the film had snapped in the projector and now nothing at all was taking place. There was stone cold silence – everything in that very moment had ceased.

What was happening? Tessa was terrified. She could barely breathe. Suddenly another arm grabbed her by the waist, and pulled her away, away from whatever clear and present danger was occurring. Through a veil of tears she looked at the sleeve; it was a uniform of some sort – then she recognized it – a policeman's blue shirt. She was being protected. But from what? Obviously, her instincts were right – this hideous man meant to harm her.

Another officer, evidently in plain clothes, had grabbed the stranger who had tried to attack her. He had him pinned against the wall. The can he had been carrying was now in the hands of one of the rescuers.

From the little Tessa could see the can was open. She learned later it was filled with lye. And she knew it was meant for her.

It was then Tessa noticed a familiar figure. Her sister Katy entered the corridor. Resplendent in her maid-of-honor gown, she looked regal, but also spoke with authority as she swiftly enlightened Tessa: "I was aware of all of this; I'd found out about the stalking. Vera told me. We were concerned for your safety. After I learned more about this Booth character – he's not too tightly wrapped – I was able to arrange for your protection. We knew he was going to try to hurt you – but for an agonizing amount of time we weren't sure just when or where. We also put on a surveillance crew at the hotel. I have to admit – since I'm personally involved – it was nerve-wracking. Thank heaven we were in time."

"Oh Katy, thank you," Tessa exclaimed, still trembling.

"You've been through a real ordeal, but from the time Vera called me – that was two weeks ago – we opened an investigation and assigned two plain clothes men to look after you," Katy explained.

"I noticed a black car parked across the street all the time; I didn't know who or what…" Tessa uttered. "I'm so glad it was the good guys."

"It didn't take much, once I looked up Ryan Booth's past history – he's long been suspected of allowing heavy drug use at his club – maybe *dealing* in it too. Then of course, there's his recently paroled brother. We knew we had a probable stalking or much worse scenario, and well, they owe me downtown and were nice enough to give me what I felt my sister needed, 24-7 protection," she explained.

Tessa looked dazed. But at least the nightmare was over.

"Here, drink some of this water," Katy offered her sister, who was clearly traumatized by the event. Tessa took the Evian bottle and quickly sipped some of it.

Her mouth was parched dry. She could barely swallow. Never mind her heart was still pounding in her chest. She still couldn't believe what had happened. It seemed to take place in a minute or less – and so quickly and quietly no one else on that hotel floor noticed or heard a thing.

"Oh Katy, I'll be forever grateful to you. I – I – "Tessa was at a loss for words.

"Please. You needn't say anything else. Just be glad we got the creep who was willing to maim you for what we believe was a putrid $10,000 fee. We knew you were being followed – that someone was told to hurt you — but we didn't know when or how until last week. That's when we got lucky and one of them agreed to turn - he'll get a plea bargain deal for identifying the others. It was Ryan Booth –you were right; he was behind it all. By last night we got wind of when the attack was going to go down. And now, you're finally safe. "

"I don't know why he couldn't let go…he's sick, very sick," Tessa sighed.

"Hey, some people are warped. Sociopaths. Psychos. I deal with them far too often. It's amazing how many of them are good looking. You can't know what goes on behind the seemingly handsome faces of serial killers like Ted Bundy.

"You're so right."

"And you just happened to come across a man with vengeance in his heart. There are those disturbed, evil sons-of-bitches who can't just move on. Look at all the wife-beatings and in too many cases, murders of women by their jealous boyfriends or controlling husbands. It's for real. The seamy side of society. A man like that – with money – and a successful night club – he could have his pick of girls – but he couldn't take rejection so he had to get to you. It's all about *Control.* From what we can tell, Booth had a rotten childhood and he never got over it. It was the mother. A lot of these men never forgive and never really like or trust women. So while he runs a hot disco club, probably could have his pick of women – your swinging the shoe at him and unfortunately breaking his nose – that did it."

"He'd slapped me hard, really hard. I finally lost my temper. He was such a prick, kept telling me to do some coke with him. I felt trapped. I shouldn't have hit him; I realized that later, but he wouldn't let me go. "

"It was self-defense, hon. You had no other choice. The fiend has a lot of demons raging inside of him. He probably wouldn't have let you go no matter what, not until he was ready. Incidentally, his brother's already been in jail twice. Now both of them are going to be up for long terms. That was lye – caustic, corrosive lye – and the beast he hired was going to toss it in your face. He could have blinded you."

"Here, let me give you a big hug," Tessa said, wiping the tears away from her eyes. The sisters embraced warmly.

"Hey now, this is your wedding day. You only have a couple of hours before the ceremony. You're going to have to compose yourself – be able to carry on without anyone becoming aware of what's happened. I know this was a terrifying experience but overall we got lucky – better that we caught them *now*" Katy said. "And Roger – his mother – our parents – nobody else has to know a thing today. They took the perp down the back stairways, so no one noticed. We asked the hotel to keep things quiet. I know they're cooperating," Katy advised. "Now go in and finish getting ready. By the way, you look beautiful."

"You don't look so bad yourself," Tessa responded, already feeling more relaxed. "Your gown is terrific!"

"Well, thanks hon, but today is *your* day and I must say everyone I've seen looks super, but you are truly radiant."

"Thank you," Tessa said, giving her sister a quick kiss on her cheek. "I'd better go back into the suite so Lance can finish my hair. Would you find Mom and tell her she's the only one who still hasn't had her face made up? I know she's been jittery, but I'm sure you can calm her down."

"Will do," Katy answered, laughing. "Mom has been fluttering all over the damned hotel. I've never seen her quite this flibbertigibberty!"

"Well it's her first daughter actually getting married and you know what a romantic she is."

"Oh my God, is she! I think she still watches the daily soap operas too," Katy smiled. "I'll go find her and we'll get the rest of the wedding party together." Katy put her arms upon her sister's shoulders and gently turned Tessa towards her; looking straight into her eyes, she said: "Tessa – just remember that whatever women do they must do it twice as well as men to be thought of half as good – fortunately this is really not difficult!"

Tessa giggled: "Touché!"

Katy was pleased for Tessa, her once saucy, overly-boy-crazy sister. Damned if she hadn't grown up and evolved into a thoughtful and caring young woman.

"A heart is not judged by how much you love; but by how much you are loved by others."

— L. FRANK BAUM, THE WONDERFUL WIZARD OF OZ

CHAPTER TWENTY-SIX

Two O'clock in the Afternoon

Tessa's heart was flip-flopping as the wedding planner placed the delicate diamond studded tiara on her head. Everything, every tiny detail was thought out, planned, discussed, decided upon and finally executed smoothly. "Thank you for making this all seem so effortless," she said to the planner.

There were still a few moments left. Tessa left the hotel suite and went up to her own room. She needed desperately to be alone. She also needed to take the time to get on her knees and pray. She had much to be thankful for on this her wedding day. *And thank the Lord that the stalking, the hang-ups, all the threats were finally over. Poor Ryan. He was a mess. She'd pray for him. He needed help, that was for sure. Dear God let this man find peace, she prayed. Tessa was relieved it was finally over. A new life awaited her.*

Finally relaxed, Tessa was relieved that aside from Katy, none of the wedding party knew what had happened. Roger would have been very disturbed, and who knows how her mother would have reacted? She was glad she could forget about it for now. She'd disclose what was necessary later. Now she would savor the day, enjoy the gift of getting married to a man she truly loved. She would always be grateful for all this joy.

Tessa was dressed as she'd always dreamed she would be. It was the most important day – so far of her life. Yet she knew the best was yet to come. She had succumbed to the Wang mystique and was wearing an ultra elegant Vera Wang custom-designed gown encrusted with delicate pearls that were hand-sewn all over its skirt, and of course, the requisite satin sling backs by Jimmy Choo on her French pedicured feet. She was soon to walk down the aisle, on her father's arm, and into the arms of her dreamy drop-dead wonderful husband –to-be, Roger Swanson. What more could a girl wish for?

"Oh darlings, everything is so beautiful," Mrs. McMullan said to her daughters as they spent the last few minutes alone upstairs. "Tessa you have done a wonderful job of planning everything beautifully. And Roger, he's such a decent young man. The way he's dedicating himself to housing the poor, it's remarkable. You must be very proud of him."

"Oh mom, he's been so gallant. When I first met him I think he was still a little bit of a playboy. But he's changed and grown and I feel privileged to know him. And as for the wedding – well Gisele suggested I hire Macy Covington – she's done so many weddings of special people – how could I miss out with a wedding planner like her? I can't take any credit for it, but I love how well everything has turned out."

"Well, so be it, you know I could have helped you – but your father and I were only too glad to pay for her services and the results are worth it – this is truly a spectacular wedding," her mother said, kissing her gently on her forehead.

Tessa was thrilled that her mother didn't have a complaint in the world. She knew she'd be pleased with the dinner yet to come – it was going to be a triumph.

The wedding dinner was to be a continuing connoisseur's banquet of high-end foods and drink to satisfy the most discriminating of gourmand preferences. Reams of caviar and foie gras along with prawns and lobster bits were brought around endlessly at the cocktail hour. The ceremony was to begin at three in the afternoon. Then would come the incredible sit-down dinner. Roger's mother took care of the orchestra as well as using her clout and money to hire none other than Tony Bennett to perform the roster of request songs from the bride and groom; besides this, she had planned an after wedding romp with the *Fab Four* to play old Beatle songs and add a dash of disco dancing to the event.

Three O'clock that afternoon –

The wedding ceremony was about to begin. Finally, Tessa felt that she had grown up. She'd long ago given up the girlishly starry-eyed fantasy of romance, yet in the end found her *Prince Charming*. And even better, she knew she was long past being thought of as other than a bubbling and bikinied beach babe – a high fashion devotee who was empty and superficial. She was going to make her mark in life – not only as the wife of Roger Swanson, but in helping him to help others. Yes, she'd like to continue to pursue an acting career, but being by his side, working on his projects for housing the poor, this was also an enormously exciting challenge and Tessa felt up to the task. At that very moment she realized that looking for love had its answer – in giving love – that in giving – love came to you.

Soon Tessa was at the entrance to the ceremonial hall, standing securely next to her father. He looked so tall and handsome in his tuxedo. The strains of Mendelssohn's *Wedding March* began as he took her arm and they walked slowly down the aisle. The guests could barely take their eyes off her; she was a knockout. All was right with the world as bliss and cheerfulness flourished throughout the wedding hall.

If you believe in true love, the union of soul mates, and happily-ever-after, then this was a wedding that was plus perfect, one with a slam-dunk happy ending. That is – until the bride stumbled ever so slightly half way down the aisle. The four-inch slim heel on her Jimmy Choo shoe had broken. It was a *sign*! A good one, she believed. It's what happened the night she and Roger had met. Wonderful! Without missing a beat, Tessa bent down, picked up the broken heel, handed it to her father, smiled, and then continued walking, a little unevenly, but beautiful as ever, she walked lopsided towards the love of her life.

The End.

No. The Beginning.

About The Author

Judi McMahon is a transplanted New Yorker who had a successful career as a newspaper reporter, editor and columnist and has authored non-fiction books published by Harper/Collins, Dell, etc. Her agent was Connie Clausen. For more than 20 years Judi wrote feature articles for newspapers and magazines in New York City, and also had her own beauty and health columns. She contributed to major magazines like New York, Redbook, Woman's Day, L'Officiel and has written more than eight how-to books. She's also appeared on talk shows; is articulate and entertaining in interviews.

Since moving to Tucson, Az., with her daughter Valentina in August of 2001, Judi has written two novels, one unpublished, the other a novelized memoir, "SOMEONE TO WATCH OVER ME," which was well-received.

Now, here for your enjoyment is her new novel: LOOKING FOR LOVE IN ALL THE WRONG AND RIGHT PLACES.

FOR CONTACT INFO:
JudiMcMahon14@Gmail.com
Telephone: 520-301-0101
or
visit Judi on her website, RebornAngel.com.

www.ingramcontent.com/pod-product-compliance
Lightning Source LLC
Chambersburg PA
CBHW071252130626
46556CB00003B/1285